THE QUEEN'S WARD

The strange death of Amy Robsart—still known
as Amy Robsart though she had been Lord Robert
Dudley's wife for some years—was the outstanding
mystery of the reign of Queen Elizabeth I. Many
believed that Amy had been murdered on her
husband's instructions, and that the young Queen
had connived at it in order that her "Robin"
might be free to marry her.

After Amy Robsart's death, Morag, the fifteen-
year-old cousin she had befriended, was taken into
the royal household, and was known as the Queen's
ward; but Morag had adored Amy, and because
Robert Dudley and the Queen had caused her
much sorrow, she hated them.

How could one so young and helpless hope to
avenge her dead cousin? Her silence was her
greatest source of power. Here is the tumultuous
love story of Morag, forced into an unhappy
marriage by royal command.

HEBE ELSNA

The Queen's Ward

Collins

FONTANA BOOKS

First published 1967
First issued in Fontana Books 1968

© *Hebe Elsna, 1967*
Printed in Great Britain
Collins Clear-Type Press
London and Glasgow

ONE

Everyone who lived within ten or twenty miles and could walk or hobble or beseech a lift in a cart, let alone the rich folk who came in their coaches or on horseback, was at the funeral. The quality as well as the poor, jostled for standing room in the churchyard. There was whispering and pulling of long faces and elbowing each other aside to see the coffin as it was lowered into the grave. Many a sidelong glance was cast at her ladyship's half-brother, John Appleyard, sombre in black even to his starched ruff, and with a drear expression which might or might not be genuine.

He was her nearest relation, it was said, and a tall, upright, proper-looking man, though several years older, he being the son of their mother's first marriage. It was no fault of Appleyard's that his half-sister, still scarcely more than a girl, had met with such a tragic end, he at the time being in his own home at Norfolk; though he may have stood to profit by her death, unless indeed Lord Robert Dudley, having as was freely said married her for her fortune, had secured all for himself.

Ah well, the sighing breath went round, it was a sad, dark business—mysterious despite the inquest finding of accidental death, or not mysterious at all if you happened to look at it in a different way. But such thoughts were only whispered, too many were in fear of Robert Dudley, who had not thought fit to attend his wife's funeral and had sent his cousin in his place.

At Cumnor Place there was much frank talk of the accident, making it seem easily brought about—a fatal carelessness, the vanity of a curved heel on a loose slipper. Those who had returned from the burying, feasted in the banqueting hall; they were too many to serve at a sitting, and they gossiped while waiting their turn. But it was careful gossiping, and for all the various suggestions as to the cause, none as much as whispered that Lady Dudley might possibly have died by ill-intent.

She had been a remote, quiet lady, a dreamer of dreams,

a lover of fine fabrics and rare jewels, not so much for the sake of wearing them, as for the touch, the possession. She had lived within the veil of her own thoughts, not one to confide or complain or to be understood. She had few to share her life, and there were few who grieved over-much for her shocking end. Indeed it was probable that of all the mourners, the only one who had truly mourned had stayed behind at Cumnor.

Morag.

The not-full-grown girl whose Cornish name this was, had for the last few days divided her time between the gazebo on the hillock in the grounds, and the alcove set in the bend of the staircase, near the great bedroom to which Amy Dudley's limp body had been carried. When conscious of hunger and thirst, she had plucked fruit from the trees in the orchard and drunk the well-water.

The alcove on the stairs was deep and dark, and although Morag wept, she was quiet there, creeping to it when the evenings turned chill. She was forgotten, as why should she not be, since only her cousin had remembered her, feeding her as often as not from her own plate ; laughing with her, that secret, soundless laughter, as she murmured: " This we will do ,Morag . . . this and that, and none else shall know of it." When Amy Dudley mingled with those others who professed perhaps more friendship than was true, she kept Morag at her side, sitting at the card table with her shining skirts spread out for the girl to nestle in. " Like a spaniel," Anthony Forster had said with his harsh laugh, and Amy, with her jewelled hand on Morag's head, had said: " She has the silken hair of such."

A freak fondness it had been considered, for Morag was a silent young creature devoid of winning ways, or, it was generally thought, of looks, though Amy had said her face was as changing and fascinating as an opal. But the silken hair was now in long strands, uncombed or brushed, and the face likened to an opal was distorted and blubbered by ceaseless tears.

Hunger for more than an apple or a pear at last drove her to the kitchen, where an immense fire roared in the grate, and the tables were laden with the remains of joints and poultry and venison pies brought out from the banqueting hall.

Distastefully, yet urged by the gnawing in her stomach, the famished girl picked out from the mêlée a small loaf of bread and a ragged slice trimmed from an aitchbone of beef. These she devoured, though, in her dry mouth, and forced down her aching throat, they were tasteless to her. She was conscious of the servants' stares fixed on her; cared nothing for them but was yet resentful. She could scarcely see out of her swollen eyes, and her thin, child's body shook as though with cold, stifling though the heat of the kitchen was on this mild September day.

The cook, stirring a syrup with an arm-long ladle, uttered a command in an undertone, and one of the scullery wenches went running, her wooden shoes clattering on the stone floor. Morag paid no attention. The gnawing pain was now appeased, as the pain in her heart could not be, and she turned to leave as silently as she came, only to find her path barred by a tall young woman, decently clad in a black dress, with her hair tucked away under a mob cap. The scullery wench stood grinning at her elbow.

"You can go," the tall girl said curtly, and dipped her head in acknowledgement to the monstrous fat cook, now supping the syrup to test its strength, and pursing her lips in doubt over it.

"Thanks, Mrs. Jolopy, and here's the angel I was told to give the one who found her, or first sent tidings of her."

The coin spun and was caught. Morag's arm was now held tightly in the older girl's grasp. She leapt away, but only so far as the other was willing to permit. From under heavy strands of light hair, big eyes gazed as through a thicket.

"Don't be frightened, Morag. Why, what's come to you that you don't remember me, Joan Brownstone? Who's scared the wits out of you, you poor moppet?"

"I'm not scared," Morag denied.

"Then so much the better. There's been those who were afeared you were lost for good and all, and made search for you. Where've you been hiding these last days?"

"I didn't hide. Anyone could have found me who cared."

"Not knowing where to look? But no matter, since you've shown yourself at last. Poor one . . . the sight you've made of your face. Her ladyship wouldn't recognise you—and she who wasn't content unless you looked perfect."

Morag's lips trembled. The food she had gulped down churned within her. She retched, her eyes glazing with horrified self-disgust, but Joan Brownstone, a kindly girl, was equal to the emergency. She dragged Morag through the kitchen door to the vegetable garden, and with cool hands pressed her forehead while she vomited.

" 'Twas the first I'd eaten, or almost, since . . ." The explanation broke off. Morag shuddered.

"And you bolted it! No wonder, though not suitable for one half-starved. It should be porridge; nothing more solid, and not too much at first."

Morag leant against the girl's shoulder, ready now to be cared for, timidly accepting kindness. Joan bore her away to the still-room, brought her the milk food. "Poor moppet, but they'll look after you," she consoled.

"They—who are they?"

"Why, who else but those who loved her ladyship as you did."

"None did." It was a sullen mutter.

"Aunt Tansy thought a deal of her, Morag. She has been beside herself—that's why you were not missed at first. Such a pother, the inquest and all, and somebody speaking up to say you might be the one to answer questions, for although she sent all of us to the fair at Oxford, you stayed behind. Then there was search for you, but you weren't found."

"How was I to know of it?"

"You were called for through the house and the gardens. Didn't you hear us calling?"

"I—don't know." But dimly she remembered the sound of her own name ringing in her ears from near and far. She had paid no attention, not supposing it to be real, but part of the nightmare. In a confused way she had believed that it was Amy's ghost voice.

"Aunt Tansy was told to see you had your decent black like all the rest," Joan said. "You can't be seen tricked out in all those fancy kirtles and petticoats her ladyship had made for you. Aunt's down at Grandma Ryman's, and like to be there till sunset, but I know where to find your black, and then I'll take you along to them who's waiting to talk to you—Mr. Appleyard—a fine-looking gentleman, and Mr. Blount, who's his lordship's own

8

cousin, and sent to take his place in mourning for her, the poor soul!"

"Nobody could take Lord Robert's place. Why didn't he come himself?"

Joan stared at the thin, pale child, who had spoken with a most unchildlike hatred and contempt. Between swollen lids there was a gleam of frosty green. Her expression was as fearless as it was miserable. Joan, in a panic that others might be within hearing, looked round apprehensively, a finger to her lips. "Have a care . . . 'tisn't for us to question our betters . . ." and then belatedly: "Though as to that, you're her kin, or so she said. Nobody rightly knew. So close her ladyship was, never explaining, even to Aunt Tansy, when she brought you home near two years ago. You wasn't one of us, but you wasn't one of them neither. Some said . . ."

But here Joan broke off, for there had been scandalous whispers, alleging that Lady Dudley's fondness for this pale elfin creature was a mother's fondness for her own child. This innuendo had only recently reached Joan's ears, and she was sure it had never been uttered in the hearing of her Aunt Tansy, who had been Lady Dudley's dressmaker and seamstress, bringing up her orphaned niece to follow the same calling. Aunt Tansy was upright and good-living, and she would have berated the scandal-mongers; nevertheless, Joan did some rapid reckoning. Poor Lady Dudley had been no more than twenty-six and married at eighteen. Morag was now over fifteen. You couldn't have a misgotten babe at eleven years old—or could you? Joan, well brought up and the daughter of pious parents, shuddered at the wickedness of her fleeting suspicion. She busied herself pulling off Morag's stained, crumpled gown, and then sponged her tear-stained face. "The mess you've made of yourself," she scolded, combing out the snarls in the lank, matted fair hair.

The black dress, simply made, with tight bodice and full skirt, was a fair enough fit, though it did nothing to disguise the child's angularity. Joan stood away to look at her. "Well, that's the best I can do, and Aunt Tansy if she were here could do no better," she said, with a pitying sigh for Morag's protruding bones.

The long table, covered with a fine velvet cloth, was

a barrier between Morag and the three men and two women who sat on the farther side of it. Except for John Appleyard and Thomas Blount she knew them all by sight, and in her cousin's lifetime they had spoken to her with careless kindness. There was Anthony Forster, Lord Robert's business agent, who had likened her to a spaniel, and Mrs. Owen and Mrs. Oddingsell, fine ladies who were his guests at Cumnor Place.

Amy Dudley had been scarcely that. A whole wing of the great house had been set aside for her, and she had arrived there on her husband's instructions some weeks before, with a large proportion of her domestic staff. She had not mingled with the others unless she so chose. She had her own cook, her own grooms and horses, and the grand-looking but extremely hard and uncomfortable coach in which she had travelled from Berkshire. She had, as Morag knew, hopefully expected her husband to join her at Cumnor.

" And is that all you can tell us, my wench?" asked Thomas Blount, a clumsily-built man who did little justice to his rich clothes. " You saw no more of your cousin than the brief glimpse of her as she bent over you in bed?"

" Not that day. I had the toothache. It had kept me awake all night. Amy rubbed my gums with—with—it was camphor, I think. She gave me a posset to drink. It had a sour taste and she—to encourage me—she took some of it herself."

Forster, who had been leaning back in his chair, cracking walnuts, which one by one he popped into his mouth, suddenly sat upright. " Mark that, sir," he said, addressing Blount, " it could be the cause of it. Who knows what was brewed? These herbal possets can be as poisonous as they are beneficial, clouding the senses."

Mrs. Owen, wife to the Queen's physician, who owned Cumnor Place but had rented it to Forster, bent forward across the table. She had a thin, sharp face, and the knuckles of the hand which played with the jewelled chain around her neck were red. Morag thought her hideous.

" So that's how it chanced!" she cried, as one who triumphs. " I remember well how she rose up in haste from the card table, saying she must see how the child did, and that was the last seen of her, until . . . Cannot you now piece it together for yourselves? Methinks she drank the posset and it made her giddy—being as like as not a brew from poppy seeds."

"It didn't make me giddy, madam," said Morag, at her most stolid.

"But you were in bed, child. You had no occasion to rise. Were you not half-asleep when Lady Dudley left you?"

"No—no . . . she stayed with me for a while—or I think she did . . . or was it that she came again to see how I fared? I can't remember." Morag choked on tears.

John Appleyard was kind. "Poor moppet! She has told you all she can, and her mind is addled."

"Why did you hide, girl?" asked Blount. "Had you seen aught to frighten you?"

"I saw—her," said Morag. "Afterwards."

Mrs. Oddingsell uttered a sharp exclamation: "Where were you then?"

"In the little room beyond hers, where I slept. I heard —noises, talk, cries, and I looked round the door, and she was carried in . . . limp. Her poor head twisted. I'd dressed myself, the toothache was gone. . . . I ran out into the garden. I wasn't sure . . . it could have been a dream."

They watched her narrowly as she put up her hands to her face, once again in tears.

"'Twas an unnatural way for any wench to act," said Mrs. Owen eagerly. "Lady Dudley had a fondness for distilling herbs, and in her ignorance might have poisoned the pair of them. The girl has been mazed, in hiding like some wild beast."

"Mazed or not," said Appleyard, "'twill be worth your while, Blount, to bring her to Windsor."

Blount nodded. "Oh aye, I'll take her along to tell her story, and perchance Robert will see significance in it. 'Tis a pity that the posset cup was cleaned. The dregs could have been tested."

"But who," murmured Mrs. Oddingsell, "would be like to think of that at the time?" Her gaze rested compassionately on Morag. "The poor maid is dropping with fatigue, and should be cared for."

"Then I commend her to your charge, sweet lady. Keep her with you for the night, and cherish her for the sake of my kinsman's gratitude. We ride to Windsor to-morrow."

Mrs. Oddingsell, who was younger, plumper and infinitely softer of manner than Mrs. Owen, rose and walked around the table to Morag's side. She put a comforting arm about her shoulders and led her away. As the door closed upon them, Mrs. Owen said:

"I doubt if 'twas well done to make so cursory a search for her. The drink was such as to so cloud the senses that it sent her to sleep forthwith, and poor Amy also partook of it. Her evidence at the inquest might have put a stop to the tongue-chattering."

"Nobody," said Appleyard, "knew that she had evidence to give, and at first it was supposed that she went to the fair with my sister's other servants."

Mrs. Owen pounced. "*Other* servants? But the girl is scarce that, is she? Amy treated her with much tenderness, and it was understood . . ."

Appleyard looked vexed. "I spoke carelessly. Morag is a relation, though a poor and obscure one . . . a distant cousin only. She was left orphaned, her mother dying at her birth after a poor marriage which the family would not acknowledge. But then Amy heard of it, and she had the child well-schooled. Two years ago, nothing would please her but to have Morag with her, and Robert, whatever the evil rumours, never denied her any wish. Morag was sent for, and was then with her constantly."

"What will happen to her now?"

Appleyard shrugged. "'Tis too soon to plan, but I shall not forget my sister's fondness for her. Poor Amy . . . if she had had children there might have been more than a mockery of a marriage."

Mrs. Owen laughed coarsely. "With the Queen's fancy set on Lord Robert, I doubt it would have made much difference, for . . ."

Blount's jerk of the head, his disapproving stare, stopped her. "Have a care for your tongue," he said.

Mrs. Owen tossed her head. "I do but hint at what the rest of the world says openly," she retorted.

The next morning when Blount and Appleyard set forth from Cumnor with their retinue, Morag rode pillion on a horse mounted by Dudley's page. Joan Brownstone had collected some of her belongings and had made them into a parcel, and a dark cloak which had belonged to Amy Dudley, fur-lined and hooded, was wrapped around her.

Morag took comfort from its soft warmth, and from the lingering fragrance of lavender with which all Amy's garments had been scented.

The page, a tall lad of eighteen, with freckles on his nose and thick reddish hair, had already spoken to Morag in the patronising way natural to his few years' seniority and his experience of court life. He made a wry face over pronouncing her name, which was one he had never heard before. His own was Guy Erskine. In some remote fashion his family was linked with that of Robert Dudley, as Morag's was linked with the Robsarts'. He assured her she need have no fear, as he could if necessary ride his horse through a tempest, and they'd keep up with the cavalcade without difficulty, the two of them being of less weight than sturdy Mr. Blount or any of his henchmen. "That's why you have been given into my charge," Guy said with boyish pride. "You're precious cargo. 'Tisn't the first time I've been trusted, though before it was with messages."

Morag did not understand him. How should she? She dreaded the journey as much as she dreaded the masked future.

"So don't you start yowling or hanging on to me too tight," Guy instructed.

"I never yowl," she said proudly.

He looked at her consideringly. "Mayhap you're not that sort, though you've cried yourself half-blind for *her*."

A poor mouse of a girl, he thought her, and there was no excitement in carrying her the thirty miles to Windsor. How different if it had been Rose Yarrow, the daughter of his mother's housekeeper, who had a smooth white neck and plump arms and yellow curls peeping beneath her cap. The village lads boasted of their successes with Rose, who was over twenty and an appetising piece. So far, Guy had done no more than yearn for her, and she had paid little attention to him, but it would be another story, he hoped, when he was next at home, after his experience at the new Queen's court.

Some miles from Cumnor, Blount and Appleyard parted company—the latter to ride to his own country home. "You will let me know what betides the wench? I have responsibility for her," he said.

"I doubt not you will be hearing from Robert himself,"

Blount replied. "You have a tender conscience for a skinny sparrow with her face the shape and colour of a lemon."

"The more in need of friends," Appleyard said, and curtly saluting the other man he rode off, with his servants following him.

The rest of the cavalcade spurred on towards Windsor. Blount had said that there was to be no pause upon the journey, which should be accomplished by nightfall.

Morag had never before ridden pillion: never before been on the back of a horse. When she had travelled with her cousin it had been by the family coach, slow, springless, entailing aching bones for a day or more after the journey, but with no sense of danger. Nobody must guess that she was now terrified. She had no right of disposal of herself, could be discarded, lifted up at the caprice of these powerful strangers; but at least she had her resolution. She would suffer in silence, her panic concealed beneath the mask of her face which the horrible Mr. Blount had said was the shape and colour of a lemon. Morag hated him for it, though she had never thought anything of her own looks, except to be glad that they pleased Amy, who had, when they were secret and alone, called her Opal. Existence until less than two years ago had been a hazard. She had been but indifferently treated by the Cornish family who had fostered her; her mother long since dead, her father dead also, having married for a second time. She had struggled through her neglected childhood with his widow's family, who had received some payment for her from the well-to-do Appleyards. And then Amy had changed all.

Morag had not understood why she was being borne to Windsor. Talk had drifted over her head, though Joan Brownstone's excitement had dimly communicated itself. She had envied Morag, who would see the great castle and perhaps some of the courtiers and ladies there in attendance on the Queen.

Now during the agonising fear and fatigue of the long journey, clutching at Guy's leather belt as he urged on his massive steed, Morag collected her thoughts, making a pattern of them. Rumour, scandal, chattering tongues, had woven a mystery about Amy's death, insisting that it was no tragic accident, but brought about by the design of her husband, whom the Queen loved and wished to marry.

14

Only Amy had stood in their way: therefore Amy must die. Lord Robert had ordered her death as the Queen might have ordered an execution, and general suspicion had fastened upon Anthony Forster, who was his business agent.

Morag hated Lord Robert because he had neglected Amy, and Amy had loved him and longed for him. Robert still cared for her, Amy insisted, but he was under a spell. The Queen was a witch, the daughter of Anne Boleyn, who had also been a witch. "But even for her sake he would not harm me." Amy, half-absently, forgetful of Morag's youth, poured random information into her ears. "'Twould do neither of them any good, for then all would rise up against her, and hate as much as they now love."

Joan Brownstone, wrapping Morag in Amy's fur-lined cloak for the journey on horseback, had explained: "They hope for you to clear her lord of all suspicion." But Morag hadn't the least inclination to serve Lord Robert's purpose. If the power were hers she would avenge those long years of neglect; and that was easy, for she need only say nothing—or nothing of any great importance.

A fleeting sensation of power touched her. Pretended dumbness, a puzzled silence, a lack of understanding . . . who could punish her for these or declare they were not genuine?

TWO

The Queen and Lord Robert Dudley paced the terrace at Windsor, not an unfamiliar sight, especially of late. Far from secluding herself from him since Amy Dudley's mysterious death, the Queen, proud and defiant, chose to single him out and to show him marks of particular favour. That he was suspected of being an assassin, a wife-murderer, was an outrage; not only that, but an arrant foolishness, for although Amy's death by some ordinary illness might have smoothed their path, the belief that it had been contrived by villainy only set them farther apart. Was it credible that the nation would tolerate as their Queen one who had connived at a rival's murder? Amy, herself saying as much, had proved her understanding of her husband and her sovereign.

On this balmy September afternoon the Queen's attendants had been instructed to keep their distance; they followed, laughing and talking among themselves. The slender young woman and the handsome Lord Robert could speak with freedom, for none were within hearing.

Strangely, these two bore some physical resemblance to each other. There was the same proud set of the head upon fine shoulders, the narrow chin, the slightly aquiline nose; but Elizabeth's large, hooded eyes had no counterpart. They were a cool grey: deep eyes which could give an effect of utter stillness, but which yet were full of life. Her mouth, perhaps her best feature, was a very feminine mouth, full and curved, though, as it was small, there was some resemblance to the petulant button that had looked so inadequate in her royal father's broad face. All such resemblance a once-despised princess had treasured, knowing well that her enemies whispered she was no true Tudor, but the child of one of Anne Boleyn's alleged lovers.

Mercifully, Henry himself had not tolerated this suspicion, cruelly though he had often treated her. She was his, even though she was the daughter who should have been a son, and the only living offspring of a woman whose wiles he had cursed. In his way he had been proud of Elizabeth's high spirit, and had thought her more beautiful than her red-gold hair and her ivory skin warranted.

Elizabeth believed in her beauty now, as she had not believed in it in those days. It had not occurred to her that she was grossly flattered when early in her reign one of her courtiers had shaded his eyes with his hand as he bowed low before her and on being questioned had averred that he was blinded by her radiance. It was he who had coined the name Gloriana, now so generally used.

Robert Dudley said: "Blount did all I bade him, followed each rumour to its source, had his men out here, out there, everywhere, listening to private talk, probing it where possible and testing the temper of those who best knew her. But he learnt little. The one, he judged, who might have given significant evidence was missing at the inquest—a girl, little more than a child, and a distant kinswoman of Amy's—devoted to her. She hid away in her fear and grief, and only crawled out of hiding when half-starved. Blount, leaving Cumnor, brought her with him, thinking that here she might be persuaded to open her clenched lips."

16

"And have you persuaded her?" the Queen asked. She had a high, light voice—unemphasised, musical.

"No—not by kindness, nor threat. She says little, though she is not dumb, and though her expression is not dull-witted. I would that you should consent to see the wench."

"To what import if I do? Robin, how often must I tell you? The mischief is done. Naught can make any difference now. Were one of God's angels suddenly to part the clouds and descend in full sight of the population to swear your innocence, and to announce that it was the will of Almighty God that I should raise you up by marriage, there would be those who would insist either that it was a hallucination, or that your well-wishers had brought about some vast trickery."

"This maid is too simple for trickery. One hour or less would convince the most sceptical of her lack of guile."

"And yet you say that she holds back?"

Lord Robert sighed impatiently. "Aye, she gives that impression, but innocently. She is in too much fear to speak freely."

"And would she not fear me? Her Queen?" This was said with arrogance.

Lord Robert had eyes of an almost womanish beauty —dark, melting, fringed with long lashes. When he turned them upon Elizabeth with adoration, and yet with a lover's mastery, it was not without effect. "Not unless you choose that she shall fear you. Your ladies worship you, and have been heard to boast that you have never given them so much as a harsh word. They love you too much to fear you . . . Bess." And then as she abruptly stood still, bringing down one elegantly shod foot on the paving stone with an unnecessary vigour: "Do not rebuke me for an allowed familiarity, dear love. I warrant those fools who walk so far behind suspect us of a more tender conversation than now takes place."

The Queen frowned. Tender words were of little value without the lover's embraces which should accompany them, and of these, ever since the news of Amy Dudley's death had reached Windsor, she had deliberately deprived herself. Lord Robert had not been banished. She had acted perfectly, giving him the sympathy a wife's sudden death merited. The ever-spreading rumour that Amy Dudley had been foully murdered, she ignored. None of her ministers, apprehensive

17

as to what action she might take, had dared to mention it to her; but although she had seen as much as ever of the man whom all believed to be her lover, she had taken care not to be alone with him, though this aloneness was what she most desired.

"I may," said Lord Robert, "have wished her death in the way that many men wish themselves rid of a wife from whom they have drifted apart, but I would not have raised a finger to bring it about."

"Have I seemed to doubt you, Rob?"

"No . . . Yes . . . you shun following the urge of your heart, though were I less scrupulous I could rouse it to such a burning fever that you would be as helpless as in an ague. You have a woman's passion, and need of me. And do not talk of raising me up by marriage, for no *man* is raised in marriage, even by a Queen."

Outraged, she flashed fury. "How *dare* you! Men have died in torture for less presumption."

"Have me arrested then—sent to the Tower—in due course to be hanged, drawn and quartered."

Betrayed by a too vivid imagination, Elizabeth was sheet-white: seeing as in some horrible vignette the ghastly tableau of block and masked executioner; the firm neck she had caressed, severed; the splendid body mutilated.

He threw back his head and laughed. "So you see you are but a woman after all."

"Yes, truly—but I have the heart of a great prince. *His* heart within this weak shell." An exquisite white hand with long, slender fingers, fleetingly rested on a bosom deliberately flattened by the fashionable, straight bodice of the day. In years to come, on an occasion more dramatically important, she was to make much the same avowal in a ringing voice to kindle all men's fervour.

"A more constant heart. Your sire sacrificed those who stood staunch to him when he most needed staunchness, and raised up many whom in jealousy he afterwards cast down. Men served him for fear, Bess, not for love as they love you. Do what you will, for you can bring them to your feet with a word."

A doubting smile slid over Elizabeth's pale face. She shook her head. "No sovereign can do precisely what he wills—not even my father—without splitting the kingdom in twain. No monarch can force subjects to accept too much. I have more care of you than you discern. My mother, God rest her soul, was set down by the people as much as by my father's change of heart. Never, I swear it, would I wreak vengeance on you whatever the sin against me, but even I cannot vouch for your safety if the populace rise against you."

"I have no fear," he said proudly.

"That I know, but I have the fear of my love for you. It behoves us to tread warily, and these are hazardous days. In the future—perchance . . ."

He shrugged impatiently. " 'Tis always so—the future —the future! One which when we were both prisoners in the Tower with our lives in jeopardy, seemed nearer to attainment than it does to-day."

"Because I was then—relatively—of small account. How would it look, think you, for the Queen to wed one whom so many judge capable of conniving at his wife's assassination? These clouds will pass, and meantime, Rob, there is much that I *can* do. Although I have no hope that this girl can change destiny by one iota, I will see her if it pleases you."

" 'Tis but a straw in the wind," he admitted, "but it crossed my mind that if the girl, so loyal to Amy, attached herself to you with an open devotion . . . could any innocent mind do that if she had reason to believe . . ."

"Not if truly innocent of self-scheming, but few are, however young." Elizabeth sighed. "Would that you had waited for me."

"What choice had I? A mere boy when the marriage was set up. My father chose brides for all his sons. A good match, so 'twas thought, with Sir John Robsart's heiress, and she mad for me, the poor fool."

There was a twinkle in Elizabeth's eyes. "You'd have thought her the bigger fool if she had not been mad for you, and she was a pretty piece. I remember seeing her once when she visited you—a prisoner—and weeping sore because she feared your doom. I pitied her—so broken down, loving much and of my own age. Who would have thought then that she would be the first to go?"

A silence fell upon them. Both still young, it was as though a full life-time of fear and craft and near-despair lay behind them. They had gazed at death too closely to have any great dread of it for themselves, though they could fear it for each other.

Elizabeth sat in a high-backed chair in one of the smaller privy rooms at Windsor. The door which opened upon this room was arras-hung and thus concealed, and without it stood an armed guard. Though fearless, the Queen was never less than well protected, and those unknown to her to whom she granted audience were searched before they were allowed within her presence. But Morag had been brought to her by Kate Ashley herself, and she, the Queen's governess when a child, was trusted as Elizabeth trusted her own right hand.

Two days ago instructions had been given to Mrs. Ashley. Morag was to be taken into her charge; she was to be fed and rested and reassured. She would be seen by the Queen only when her nervous tremors were stilled. "You will be very kind, Ashley," said Elizabeth, adding with the smile of confidence and affection that others rarely saw: "As only you can be kind."

Mrs. Ashley, middle-aged, fussy, maternal, had done her best. Morag was no longer the forlorn-looking waif who had stood at the kitchen table at Cumnor, thrusting bread and meat into her starved mouth. She wore a black dress, but it was not made of the rough cloth which had been doled out to those of Amy Dudley's household. Mrs. Ashley had procured one from the extensive wardrobe at Windsor, where there were garments of all description. Skilled fingers had altered it to fit Morag; cut square at the neck, it was relieved by big sleeves of white lawn. There were buckles on her black leather shoes, and a gold chain which had been one of Amy's gifts hung around her throat. Her fair hair was tucked neatly beneath a white cap with starched wings. "Curtsy to Her Grace," Mrs. Ashley had commanded, and she had done so with an unexpected composure. Now she stood with bent head before her Queen. Mrs. Ashley at a gesture from Elizabeth had left them.

The Queen said: "They tell me your name is Morag —what else?"

"Trevenna, may it please Your Majesty."

"A Cornish name, but your mother was—a Robsart? You and Lady Dudley were cousins?"

" 'Twas a distant relationship, Your Grace. I do not know how distant, only that when my mother married my father, her family let her go and saw no more of her. It was long after she died, long after my father had married again, that Amy heard of me, and asked Lord Dudley if she might have me to live with her."

" And Lord Dudley was willing? That was a kindness on his part, was it not?"

Morag muttered an assent which might have been sullen or unwilling or merely shy. From beneath lids that were still faintly pink with the weeping of past days, she shot a glance at the slender figure in the throne-like chair. So this was Anne Boleyn's daughter. It was thus she thought of Elizabeth, for Amy in resentment had rarely referred to her as the Queen. A witch's offspring, Amy had said, who would bring no good fortune to England, nor on any upon whom she cast her spell. Anne Boleyn had had five fingers and a thumb on one hand—a little, useless finger, so it was said, and a sure sign that she was a witch. There was no such disfigurement on the slender, jewelled hands of the Queen. Morag had never seen hands so perfect. Dreamily her mind memorised them; unconsciously the forefinger of her own right hand traced upon the palm of her left, the exquisite shape.

"What do you?" The Queen watched her with narrowed eyes.

Morag started guiltily. "Naught, Your Grace."

"It was as though you drew."

Morag shook her head: "I cannot draw." And then, slowly, as though the words were dragged from her: "I did—in my mind—but model Your Grace's hand."

"Can you do that, then—modelling?"

"I have tried. Amy thought—she said—it was a natural talent."

Tears once more steeped Morag's eyes; but Elizabeth's eyes were alert with a new interest; the interest that would always be aroused by the unusual, stimulated by beauty or talent or wit. For a startling moment she envied Amy Dudley with a new envy, not because of the husband who had tired of her, who while bound to her had chafed at the bond, but because of the absolute love with which she had inspired this strange child. All England was said to love the Queen, but would any so grieve at her death? Yet

21

Robert had said that Amy was stupid—a pretty dunce who palled on all who knew her, through her dullness; a barren wife whose love cloyed and whose extravagance in clothes and jewel-buying would have been the ruination of a poor man. Could she have been all this and yet be so adored, even by one person?

"Come sit here on this cushion near to me," said Elizabeth. "Tell me of your life with her."

Nothing could have been further from Morag's wish, but the Queen must be obeyed, and the Queen had charm, which when she chose to exercise it, few could resist. Morag sat on the cushion, and the Queen said: "I would look at you more closely, take off your cap." Trembling hands removed it, and Elizabeth noted them as Morag had noted hers. A child's hands—unbeautiful—with stubby fingers and bitten nails. She must be cured of that, thought the Queen, in the governess mood with which her maids of honour were already acquainted. But all she now said was: "A talent should be cultivated. You know the Bible parable?"

"Yes, Your Grace. Amy said—she said . . ."

"I warrant she promised you the opportunity to cultivate it. To do as much or more than she could for you, would be an honourable memorial to her. I would I had known her, but I saw her once only, from a distance."

From a barred window as Amy, the visitor, had been let out through the grim gates: a fair and pretty girl who had gazed back yearningly at the fortress where her young husband was imprisoned.

"Tell me about her," said Elizabeth. "Was she very unhappy? So unhappy that she might have taken her life?"

"Never—she never would." The small head with its braids of fawn-coloured hair was vigorously shaken, and then came the lie to save the pride of a dead woman: "She was not unhappy."

"But I heard, I have been told, that she was restless, moving from house to house, unable to settle, lonely because her lord was at court and she saw little of him."

"He would soon have been with her again. He had promised. She trusted him. She knew that he owed duty to Your Grace and must fulfil it, but he wrote that he was eager to be with her. I saw the letter. When she slept at nights it was beneath her pillow."

Elizabeth bit her lip. Then it was a lover's letter, for it was only such that women thus cherished. Could Robert indeed have employed such duplicity? But the child was too ignorant of what was between him and his Queen to lie to her. Had he after all deluded the wretched woman, and in some subtle way encompassed her death? Yet when he had sworn innocence, she—Elizabeth—had believed him.

Questions came swiftly and were at first haltingly answered. Later they were glib. Elizabeth heard of that last day—of the herbal concoction that Amy had brewed—a posset so bitter that Morag had pushed it aside, and then Amy had sipped it and had said it was hardly bitter at all. Elizabeth knew that this was the statement which to Anthony Forster, to Thomas Blount and to John Applegate had had significance. They had sought with craft to induce Morag to amplify it. "Did she drink much of the posset?" Elizabeth asked.

"I don't know . . . they asked me that . . . I don't know. I was in pain and Amy was disappointed because of the fair. She thought that if the pain went we could still go there."

"She wanted to go—with you—to the fair at Oxford, whither she had sent her servants?" To the Queen it sounded strangely undignified. Amy, after all, however badly treated, had been a great lady.

"It was for a jest, a secret thing between us. I was to dress as a boy, and she as a man in doublet and hose, with a pointed beard and a slouch hat. We could pass as father and son, she said, and she would win her wager that she could go there and return unseen."

"With whom did she wager this?"

"She didn't tell me, only laughed and said she would show him her mettle, that she had no fear and that she could act a part. But I had been awake all night with the toothache, and she would not go without me."

A prank, a hoydenish prank, mused the Queen. Who had sought to lead Amy Dudley into such foolishness, and for what purpose? Had there been some foul intent behind it? If so, Amy had but escaped it to meet a different but no less deadly fate. She was not the only one who had suffered, Elizabeth mused; this child was as bereft as though she had lost her mother. Few guessed the touching appeal that any such orphan held for Elizabeth. She never spoke of her own mother, but there was scarcely a day in which she had not thought of her. Throughout the years she had asked few questions, but as a child she had heard snatches of conversation not meant for her ears.

Just as vivid as the vignette in which the man she loved met a violent death from her enemies, she could image the vignette of her mother's real and cruel death, the pride and courage with which she met it, the masked executioner sent from France with the great sword warranted to give a deposed Queen a painless end . . . not the hacking brutality that had been Thomas Seymour's fate. Baby though she had been when she had last seen her mother, she was sure she remembered her. The smile that transformed into beauty the face that had bent over her, the peal of her laughter as fat, baby hands had clutched at a dangling toy. She had learnt, early, at Mrs. Ashley's bidding, to subdue her own tendency to wild laughter, even on the rare occasions when her royal father condescended to visit the nursery and she was allowed to frolic with her little brother. As she passed beyond early childhood, she had known instinctively that it was because this laughter reminded Henry of her mother. He never forgot her, thought Elizabeth proudly, and neither do I.

It seemed to her that there was an analogy between Anne Boleyn and Amy Robsart: both redundant, to their husbands. But Anne's life had not been purposeless. Although she had borne only one child who had lived, a girl child, that child was now the Queen. Mary Tudor in her rages had called Anne "Whore," and once, hearing this, Mrs. Ashley in her indignation had put her arms about the proud, stricken Elizabeth, and out of Mary's hearing had murmured that it was a foul calumny. Anne had been gay and vivacious, but never less than true. "Pray for her," Mrs. Ashley had said. "She loved you, and she watches over you, and she will bring you to power and glory." And so she had, just as dear Kate Ashley had promised, thought the Queen, once more giving her attention to the girl who sat on a cushion at her feet.

Jane Seymour had no more wanted Anne's death than Elizabeth had wanted Amy's. In her brief life she had shown nothing but kindness to Elizabeth, and to Catherine of Aragon's daughter. Elizabeth was in love with Robert Dudley, but did she actually want to marry him? She

24

had had her moments of doubt, and now Amy's death had set up an impassable barrier. It could not be. England and her Queenship came before all else. I will reign alone, thought Elizabeth proudly. All I can give him, I will, but not that—not that. . . . And she would be kind to this forlorn young creature whom the childless Amy had mothered.

She stooped to finger the gold locket that swung on the chain about Morag's neck. "Is it her face within?" she asked, but when Morag uttered the assenting word, she did not open the locket.

The child might know more than she had told. Lord Robert had believed that she held something back, and the same suspicion glanced across Elizabeth's mind. But she was content that it should be so. Complete and open vindication of her lover, if by any extraordinary chance Morag could provide such vindication, not knowing it was in her power, might not, after all, serve the Queen's purpose.

Her people would have her wedded, but not to Lord Robert Dudley, the only man who had stirred her blood since Thomas Seymour had loved her in her adolescence. A dastardly love, for he had been Katherine Parr's husband, and Elizabeth had been fond of Katherine, who had shown her endless kindness. In that first youth she had been weak, but never, never again. It would be less sacrifice than for most women. Pride reared at the thought of a husband's dominance, and her slender, perfect body shrank in revulsion at the prospect of child-bearing. Her mother had suffered hideously, she had heard. Jane Seymour had died, and so had Katherine Parr. It was better, far better, to belong only to oneself, set above others by her virginity as well as her Queenship. Amongst the throng of pretty creatures who were called the Queen's maids there might be venial huzzies, and to them she would be unrelenting, but to those who loved and obeyed, she would be kind.

"You are not alone," she told Morag. "You were her ward, but now you are the Queen's ward, and none shall harm you." A slim hand was stretched forth and Morag kissed it. Amy, thought Morag, would have done the same, but she would have done it with hatred in her heart. Amy could not be sure if she hated the witch's daughter. She was too bemused.

THREE

When one is young, time slips away smoothly, swiftly, generally unregretted. The future appears to offer prizes which in the past and present are unobtainable. For Morag there was a year or more lost in a virtual bewilderment. Her status was unresolved. She was not one of the Queen's accredited ladies, though Elizabeth had announced openly that she was her ward. She was not sent to Hatsfield or Hunsden, but given into the charge of Mrs. Ashley, who in her turn had her lodged with one of the Queen's more elderly dressers, who was a widow with no children of her own.

She learnt Greek and Latin and modern languages. She was instructed in the Protestant religion, encouraged to take an interest in theology. Her childish handwriting changed to a script of elegant fluency. She was taught to play the virginals, and developed a love of reading. The great library at Windsor was open to her. Roger Ascham, who had been the Queen's tutor, now supervised Morag's studies and reported to his royal mistress, who, hearing that Morag was especially intelligent, took the greater interest in her.

Modelling in clay and wax was a definite talent, but in this there was nobody to give her specific instruction, and she resisted the Queen's suggestion that she should experiment with wood carving. This wax modelling, the Queen decided, was more in the nature of a diversion than a compulsive ambition. Morag was reluctant to display her efforts, though she produced a model of the late Edward VI which startled Elizabeth because it was so lifelike, though Morag had had only a miniature portrait to guide her. It seemed singular to the Queen that Morag could neither paint nor draw; with pencil or brush she was inept.

"It is little more than a game to her," Elizabeth told Lord Robert one day when they were alone together. "Yet there is a strange, facile talent. She has dressed this puppet out of odd scraps of silk and velvet, and one could almost expect to see it move and talk, though 'tis no more than a foot in height. But the girl has a singular attitude towards this gift of hers—she has not the enthusiasm of one who

26

has a vocation. But then enthusiasm is what she lacks generally in all her studies, bright-brained though she is."

Lord Robert did not think it in the least singular. So many children had seeming gifts, such as composing verses or painting scenes from nature, which vanished as they attained maturity. The Queen was a natural scholar; all the royal children had been noted for their industry and their intellectual prowess. Little had it profited them. Mary Tudor's theological knowledge had been corroded by bigotry; Lady Jane Grey's learning had not saved her from acting like a little fool. If she had had the wit to refuse to allow the crown to be placed upon her head, refused for a brief nine days to accept the status of Queenship, her head would still be on her shoulders, and she probably alive. Her intellect had not endowed her with common sense. Mary would have spared her had she not been a usurper, however unwilling. As for Edward, he, in frail health, had been literally sacrificed to his books. Elizabeth's shrewdness, the agility with which she had baffled Mary, her knack of avoiding danger, had been of far greater value to her than her skill at embroidery and her knowledge of modern languages.

"Maids of Morag's age are dreamers," he said, "and she more than most has found alleviation in dreaming and solitary play. She has had a hard and uncertain life with many changes. This is the second time she has been spirited into a strange world. Were you not set on her, she could be apprenticed and taught the trade of doll-making."

"But these models are more than dolls, Rob. They take a deal of time and labour to produce. Morag was weeks over the figure of poor Edward. It would be of no interest to her to make simpering, pretty dolls with painted cheeks and flaxen wigs. She has something more, to which at the present I cannot give a name. . . . There is an oddity, for she said the other day that although she could only model real people, she preferred them to be dead people. I could not coax a reason from her."

Dudley, who had no great interest in Morag as an individual, said chillingly: "I wish I could be sure, Bess, that you have shown wisdom in keeping her with you."

Elizabeth frowned, for some of her ministers, notably Cecil, had hinted the same thing.

"But it was you who brought her to me, thinking that if she, so bound to your wife by love, came to show an equal devotion to me, it would demonstrate that the foul stories concerning Amy's death and your complicity, were set at naught by the one who had been closest to her."

"I had many confused thoughts at that time, and did not suppose her presence here would be permanent. Now 'tis a two-edged sword."

"I do not understand you. What possible harm can there be in the poor child?"

"No conscious harm, but has it not struck upon you that it may be said you have made her your ward in order to seal her lips? She is secluded from the maliciously curious who might question her."

"I have questioned her. You have questioned her, as did others before she arrived here, and she could tell nothing."

"That is not generally known. There are, I doubt not, those who say that two courses were open to you. The girl could have been done away with by stealth, by some natural-seeming accident; or there was the humane safeguard of befriending her, winning her love and insuring her silence."

The Queen bit her lip with anger: "Can one not perform an act of charity without any such devious cause? It is not the first time I have befriended the weak and the helpless."

"Oh, my love, do I not know it, but those of evil intent are wont to be incredulous."

"I do not brook dictation, nor shall I alter my ways for those who can be only despised."

Dudley shrugged. "I know full well that you will not. To warn you is vain, yet it behoved me to do so as my duty. Every man is urged to protect the woman he loves from ill-speaking, be she Queen or peasant."

"Fortunately, as I am Queen, I can exact retribution for ill-speaking. Should any such come to my ears, the knave's tongue shall be slit." And then Elizabeth said, almost wistfully: "I have a fondness for the maid. She has a quiet gentleness that soothes me, and unlike others I have favoured, she asks nothing for herself. The money with which I fill her purse is either unspent or given to the first beggar who entreats her. She would wear the same gown month in month out, did I not instruct Kate Ashley to see she has all that befits her. I could send her abroad to Holland to study under Van Eyton the sculptor, who has, I hear, set up a school in Amsterdam; but if I have a weakness Robin, it is in my wish to keep about me those for whom I have an affection. Nobody knows that better than you."

"You are lonely, Bess, as you would not be if you soldered the link between us."

"Might it not be a link galling to your pride? Would it please you to be known as my husband, but with no power? Even if I sign a patent raising you to an earldom, your rank will be far less than mine."

"Sweeting, it is within your power to do more. A queen can raise her consort to be king."

"Ha!" Elizabeth fixed him with an arrogant gaze. "So now 'tis out. Your ambition knows no bounds, my lord!" White with anger, her half-raised hand suggested that in another second she would smite him across the face, but Lord Robert caught it in his.

"You know me better, Bess. A king can be a puppet. Has not history proved it so? I am ambitious only for your openly acknowledged love. The very air about us stirs and hums with the rumour of your betrothal to this foreign prince or that, but think before it is too late. Can you do better than give the country an heir who is English in every fibre of his being?"

The Queen's face became blankly expressionless, as it so often did at a reference to her possible child-bearing. "In sooth we might have no children," she said. "Your wife had none."

Dudley regarded her with amusement. "Amy was not the only woman I bedded," he said crudely, "and there have been sons by others—more than one fine boy who in looks is a Dudley, though he has no claim to use my name."

"And yet you say you love none but me."

"Dear heart, 'tis true, but the sowing of my wild oats were in the years when you were immured at Hatfield, and I for months on end saw naught of you. Amy, poor soul, was not one to set the heart afire, and she was of a frigid humour, whereas I am a man who has ne'er pretended to be of monkish tastes."

Elizabeth sighed, longingly as it seemed to him. He

went swiftly to the door of her apartment and turned the key in the lock. She watched him in silence, and when he took her in his arms she yielded to him. Dudley's hopes soared. Could he but bring her to the point when she was in a fever to be ravished by him, all might end as he desired. With child by him, she could no longer refuse to marry him.

But even as he held her in his arms and was permitted to fondle her, he knew that she was either incapable of complete surrender, or that her will was too strong to suffer it. There had been several of these promising scenes, in which she had been half-swooning with desire for him, but had drawn back at the ultimate moment, reproaching herself for her weakness, and him for being eager to take advantage of it. But there was *no* weakness in her, he thought sourly, the prize was dangled before him as a carrot before a donkey. There were occasions now when he wearied of the pursuit, desirable though she was to him.

Morag had modelled the Queen's hands—a task which had given her considerable satisfaction, since she was sure they were the most beautiful hands in the world. Now with the wax cooled and hardened, they were set out on a velvet-covered tray. Pale hands, gem-adorned, clasped a book. Slender hands, long-fingered, were raised in prayer. Idle hands rested with palms upturned.

The Queen examined the various models with interest. Vanity was gratified. Morag, praised, was told that on no account must this work be destroyed. A glass case should be made in which the models could be displayed.

"I have a plan devised for you," Elizabeth said. "Years ago, though it has now fallen out of custom, my father had a jester—a fool attached to his court who lightened his despondent hours. Before that again, there was a puppet master, who in his own midget theatre would give performances of the Greek tragedies, with his puppets manipulated by wires, and actors declaiming the great speeches. I have a mind to revive this art, for art it was, and who should make the puppets better than you?"

"But I could not make them act, Your Majesty," said Morag with alarm.

"Not to act, mayhap, but you could be taught the

rudiments of anatomy. Then each limb could be modelled separately and jointed."

Morag shook her head. "Madam, I doubt that I could master such a craft. It is as though my hands make a portrait, but only of a face with perchance some special feature added thereto, such as hands or feet, if these be noteworthy. I cannot devise the modelling of a body. When dressed, it is not noticeable that my puppets possess only shapeless stems. Nor can I devise a face from imagination. It must be actual."

The Queen was not to be denied. "No matter. We will provide you with sitters, and you must practise the jointing, so that a puppet can bow or dance or fall in a swoon, or perform other such contortions. There are still those who give crude shows at fairs, or so I have been told."

"But I work slowly, and if I could learn this process, it would take weeks, months, to make so many models."

"Put off with no further excuses, child. I have already heard of one who can instruct you. As for time—of that there is sufficient. All the long autumn and the winter before you. But on Twelfth Night it is my will that in addition to the Masque, which is of no novelty to anyone at court, there should be this puppet play. Before then, a producer will be found. As for models, are there not courtiers and ladies in abundance to provide you?"

Elizabeth could scarcely have accounted for her own persistence. She was restless for novelty. Nowadays there was a constant influx of Continental visitors—ambassadors who schemed for a marriage between her and the various princes and monarchs they served. The glitter of her brilliant court was Elizabeth's pride. It was, and must continue to be, the wonder of the world, with handsome courtiers circling around the magnificent centre-piece, which was the Queen: virginal, proud, though gracious.

Morag's lack of ambition to rise in her favour, her retiring spirit, endeared her to Elizabeth, and yet it baulked her. It was as though no prize her royal patron could offer was of importance to her.

"Sometimes I could believe your true home is in a convent," she said vexedly.

But to this, Morag shook her head. "Oh no, Your

Grace. For one thing, I am not Catholic, and for another, how one's knees would ache with so much kneeling, and one's voice tire of chanting prayers."

The Queen laughed. "You shall tire in another fashion. Next week we move to Greenwich, and there is a banquet and a ball to be given for the Spanish Ambassador. You shall be there, and in a new gown—you are old enough to enjoy a ball. As for your first model—a good choice might be that stripling who has dangled after you of late—Guy Erskine."

"I might be able to make a model of Guy," admitted Morag.

It was true that she disliked taking her models from those who lived, preferring to copy a painting or a statue, but she was relieved because the Queen had selected one with whom she was at ease. She had a mild liking for Guy, who was her contemporary and treated her with a teasing friendliness that she could match.

"He is a well-set-up lad," said Elizabeth. "See what you can do with him."

Morag, when she was alone, pondered over this new fancy of the Queen's, and also pondered a little over her own reluctance. She did not know when or where it was she had heard that to model a living being in wax brought ill fortune to them, but the fear that it might be so, spoiled her pleasure in such work. Hands were different, she told herself ; they were not a whole person, and even the figures she had moulded in wax and then dressed elaborately, stitching silk and velvet upon them, were not whole, for as she had told the Queen, they were, from the neck down, whether a model of man, woman or child, quite formless. But such puppets as the Queen now desired to see produced must be formed, and with all her being she shrank from such work. All she could do to protect herself and to convince Elizabeth of her inability was to produce grotesque shapes that resembled nothing human ; and that she would, whatever instructor might be provided for her.

This promise Elizabeth did not forget. The next day an elderly leech, bowing and subservient, waited upon Morag. Once he had been a surgeon of some repute, but he was now in his late seventies and had long since retired. The Queen's retentive memory had fastened upon a day when she had heard two of her maids of honour giggling, with pretended shuddering, because they had heard from some village talk that Dr. Jebb in his dining-room had the skeleton of some unknown man. It was his humour to have the skeleton dressed in doublet and hose and velvet cloak, and seated at table with him. An old Roman custom, he had told a new housekeeper when she had shuddered and remonstrated. They must ever remember, said Dr. Jebb, that even in the hour of greatest prosperity, death was lord of all, and would finally claim each one of them. But his young housekeeper, replacing an old woman who would have given no heed to half a dozen skeletons, had no mind to remember any such thing, and throwing over her situation, she had spread it far and wide that her master was mad or possessed of the devil. Henceforward he had been served by a surly manservant, for no woman was to be found who would live under his roof.

Recalling this story, Elizabeth had sent for Dr. Jebb and questioned him. Overwhelmed, the old leech admitted that all told of him was true; admitted also that he knew more of anatomy than was usual to a country apothecary. The Queen had promptly said that he was to give such instruction as he could to Morag. The puppets she made must be flexible and jointed, and that was an art that could be learnt.

The leech did his best, but Morag, stubborn, would have baffled any such tutor. She was as superstitious as she was unwilling, and one day when Guy Erskine looked in at the door of her schoolroom she was near to tears. Before her on the table was a great coil of wire, and diagrams of a human skeleton of about the same length as her foot-high puppets.

"So it is true, all this talk of turning you into a puppet-maker," Guy said. "I could scarce believe it. What then does possess the Queen?"

"The desire for a novelty," said Morag wearily. "There are to be great revels at Twelfth Night, and before then, not only a score of puppets contrived, and a showman to pull the strings, but a play especially written, and actors from the playhouse to speak the lines. Did not the Queen give orders that you were to be the model for the first puppet?"

"She said I must be at your disposal, an order which pleased me well enough. When do you start on this work?"

"When I have mastered this new conception of it, which

will be never. I dare not openly defy the Queen, but Dr. Jebb will help me, I think. He agrees that 'tis unseemly for a maid realistically to produce in wax the human figure, and will suggest it to Her Grace."

"Would that indeed affront your modesty?" Guy inquired.

"I dislike it, but not for the sake of modesty. I will not do it, and I wish now that the Queen had not discovered I had this facility for producing a likeness in wax, of which she makes so much."

"I doubt if wax is a good medium for jointing," Guy said. "There are strolling showmen in plenty to make a jointed body in wood; and to that your wax heads could be affixed, giving them the human likeness, instead of a daubed wooden face. The Queen would agree to that, perchance."

"Oh, if she only would! If you could suggest it to her!"

"Why not? Between us, Dr. Jebb and I should be able to work upon her. I will do my best, and then will sit for you, Morag. 'Twill be less tedious than many of the senseless duties foisted upon a court page."

"Do you find it tedious at court? To me it seems one ceaseless whirl of pleasure, and all the time something new—fresh, as the Queen demands."

Guy shrugged. "I would fain be my own master, acting as land agent to my father, and so it might have been, though my father is loth to give me authority, had I not been bound to Dudley. My mother," said Guy, making a wry face, "is ambitious. Moreover she has, though a woman of all the virtues, a softness for my lord Dudley, and thought it an honour when he tok notice of me. Little she guessed the danger of it. While Queen Mary reigned, I acted as messenger between him and the Lady Elizabeth. 'Twas hazardous, but worth it for the excitement."

"What did you have to do?" asked Morag, her great eyes fixed on him and her heart fast beating. Did he mean that he had carried love-letters to Elizabeth while Amy was still alive?

"To do? To warn her, of course, you simpleton. Time and again while she was lodged at Hatfield she knew not which way to turn for safety. There were those who would have lured her on the pretence of joining Queen Mary, to partner Wyatt on his march to London. There

34

were those who would have had her believe the Queen when ailing was already dead, would have set an imitation crown upon her head and brought her to London as though to usurp the throne, knowing full well that that would bring about her beheading as a traitor. My lord Dudley, hearing of these schemes, sent messages by me to warn her to trust nobody, and to remain where she was. I was the least likely of any to be suspected, since my home Linksfields is not far from Hatfield. What more natural than that an only son should pay frequent visits to his family? 'Twas a stroke of luck when the weather was stormy, for who was likely to pursue one who rode through blinding rain or sleet? At first I carried messages written on scraps of paper, rolled into tiny pellets; but at the last, when my lord was sure of me and my memory, and the Lady Elizabeth trusted me, they were by word of mouth."

"Truly the Queen owes you much."

"She says so, and thus has filched me from Lord Robert to follow in her train. An honour, though it is often wearisome."

"I am astonished you find it so, for most often when I see you, you are surrounded by languishing ladies listening to your lute-playing and your songs."

He grinned at this tartness. "'Tis true that most of your sex are kind."

"You should have a care, Guy. The Queen, herself a maid, is insistent that hers should be so in more than name."

Guy observed her with interest. "You have become mighty shrewd of late. Yet 'tis less than two years since you were a shivering little whippet, terrified of riding pillion to Windsor. How come you by such understanding? You mingle with others but rarely, and have no mind for gossip."

Morag shrugged. She did to an extent understand the Queen, but she could not have said from where she had derived such understanding.

"She is not beautiful," mused Guy, "yet she has the courage to brave the contrast when she surrounds herself with beauty."

"She has more than beauty. She does not need it." Morag uttered this tribute with reluctance. Even now she could not tell whether she loved or hated the one who had been the cause of such tribulation to her adored Amy.

"'Tis true! That elegance—those eyes that can be of

35

several colours and hold all the light—that arrogance. Who can challenge it?"

"Nobody. She is the Queen, and a queen *should* be arrogant—and humble," said Morag.

"Because she denies herself, she would deny gratification also to her ladies. That is why she calls them her wards, and considers it her right to guard them. But as is natural, they cheat her. Behind the demure smiles and downcast eyes . . ." Guy broke off to laugh with self-satisfaction, and Morag flashed him an antagonistic glance, her womanhood resenting his male confidence.

To her there was nothing particularly attractive about the young man who sat on the edge of the table, swinging his long legs, yet there was an innate satisfaction in the knowledge that of late Guy, who was so smiled upon by the maids of honour, had shown that he found her interesting, and made opportunities to be alone with her. She knew that her appearance had greatly altered, and would have been inhuman had this not been a pleasure to her. Her pathetic boniness had vanished, and now she had graceful curves, small, high breasts, a creamy skin. Her fawn-coloured hair was abundant, and her greenish-grey eyes were large, thick-lashed and tantalisingly cool. She was above medium height.

"To-night there is to be a ball for the Spanish Ambassador, and you will be there," Guy said. "I was in waiting on the Queen when she sent for old Ashley and told her you were to be fitted for a new gown, and that was a week ago. Is it a becoming gown, sweeting?"

"Oh, yes. Of cream taffeta with a pearl embroidery. Not that I have need of new gowns. All that my cousin possessed, and she had a quantity, were passed on to me by Lord Dudley's orders. Many have been altered for me."

"But you must weary of wearing clothes that were the property of another woman—and she dead."

"Some of them were unworn, and I prize them," Morag said.

"How true you are to her through your love. 'Tis a rare quality, for most women change about as weathercocks. One day you will love and marry, and your husband will prize such constancy."

"Will he?" Guy mattered little, and yet she felt slightly

dazed. It was the first time that any man had put his hand over hers in that possessive way. Holding it down firmly, pinned to the table beneath his own.

"If he's the same brand of man that I am," Guy said.

She laughed, but there was a quiver in the laughter. "You would find it tedious."

"Never. A man has to settle—and with me it will soon be time. I have a duty to Linkfields and no younger brother to step into my shoes. But for that, I might have gone to Holland—France—Italy, joined the army there, but that makes my mother weep. She appealed to the Queen, who when she was the Lady Elizabeth was friendly with her. In those days she was glad of friends—at Hatfield. Now the Queen has issued her commands. She has need of me here—one day there will be other plans for me, she says. . . . Morag, you are not a child any longer."

"No. I was seventeen a month ago."

"And I knew it not. If I had . . . poor sweeting, there should have been a present for you." He took a jewelled pin from his tunic, one of several, though none of great worth. This was an opal, set about with small pearls. He bent forward and fastened it to the bodice of Morag's gown. "A keepsake," he said.

"Guy, I cannot take it!"

"My poppet, the Queen's maids are accustomed to such gifts; they are a commonplace, and sometimes from those who scarce know them. It is a slight thing, Morag."

"Amy called me Opal," she said, not knowing why she told him.

"She valued you—and rightly. And she did well by you. Has nobody told you?"

"Told me what?"

"She left you a dower. My lord Dudley was agreeable to it. She was, after all, responsible for you. You won't be a penniless bride, my pretty one."

Morag's eyes filled with tears. "She thought of everything."

"Don't cry—though shining tears but make your eyes the lovelier."

In another moment he would kiss her. Morag drew back from him, and as she did so, Mrs. Ashley bustled in, the new cream gown over her arm.

"One last fitting," she said, her keen gaze travelling from Morag's flushed face to Guy's.

He swung his long legs to the ground, and moved leisurely towards the door. He was amused by Morag's confusion and by Kate Ashley's suspicious gaze. "Until this evening, sweeting," he said, and was gone.

The Queen, he knew, would hear of this encounter from Mrs. Ashley, who told her everything, even the merest tittle-tattle. She might or might not be displeased, but Morag could not be kept in cloistered innocence for ever. As for himself—as Morag had said, Elizabeth owed him something, and why not a bride? Docile, innocent, dowered, and blooming with an unusual prettiness. He might do worse, Guy reflected. A man should marry and found a family, and Morag would be an undemanding wife: an unsuspicious wife. The Rose Yarrows would always be to his taste, who relished a spice of coarseness and greedy passion, but Morag was another Amy Dudley, patiently enduring neglect; a useful asset in the background; the bearer of sons. She would neither ask nor expect more than he was willing to give.

FOUR

At the great ball given for the Spanish Ambassador, Guy Erskine was not the only one to notice Morag, who suddenly, unknowingly, had acquired a star-like quality. It was not only the new gown, though that was becoming, giving her a young dignity. It was the consciousness of being a child no longer. She could almost have believed herself in love with Guy, because he had singled her out, had made her feel that she was desirable—the sweetest emotion of all, to the young and unconfident. And there was the new knowledge of Amy, who had thought of her, and although young and with no expectation of death, had provided for her future. Amy had loved her—wonderfully. The only person who ever had, thought Morag. She did not make the mistake of thinking that the Queen loved her, though she was often kind, even caressing. Morag did not believe that the Queen could really love anyone, anything, except England.

She glanced across the great hall to where Elizabeth sat on her throne-like chair of red velvet stamped with her initial in gold. A spontaneous understanding welled up within Morag; a strange, new emotion which contracted her chest, clutched at her throat. She could not bear to tear her eyes away from that slim figure in its magnificent, gem-shimmering stomacher and enormous quilted skirt. There were pearls, ropes of them about Elizabeth's throat, and threaded in and out of the meshes of her flame-coloured hair. The stillness, the arrogant poise, of Elizabeth's body was more impressive than her animated face, which she turned first to one who stood beside her, and then to another.

She is great, thought Morag. She is beyond imitation, she is more than just a woman. Why *should* she love anyone when we are all so far beneath? She is England.

With the unuttered words there came a sense of release. Elizabeth had never really loved Robert Dudley, therefore Elizabeth could be forgiven. An ordinary woman, thought Morag, even though a queen, put love first. Flattering courtiers spoke of Elizabeth as a goddess to send men mad. It was a stupidity. A goddess would probably have a chilling effect on a human being, but Elizabeth shed warmth upon all her subjects, because they were part of her great country.

Dancing came easily to Morag, and that evening she danced more than once with Robert Dudley as her partner, and stood by him in a group, listening as the Queen played the virginals and sang sweetly enough. Morag slipped away presently to walk on the terrace. It was a warm, still, moonless night, and although she could see nobody, she occasionally heard a stifled giggle, sigh or whisper. Presently, a hand was on her shoulder. "The Queen asks for you," said Robert Dudley. "I saw you glide out through the side door and said I would fetch you. Unlike the other maids you do not seek the dark with a partner, but stand in the light streaming from the window. How is't that Guy Erskine has let you escape—alone?"

"He has others to divert him, and owes no duty to me," said Morag, very conscious of the hand that now seemed to press heavily upon her shoulder. In the muted light from the window behind her, she could only hazily see the handsome face of which Amy had spoken with such wistful tenderness. Morag could not deny its confident charm; the smile which was half-mocking and yet gentle; the dark softness of the eyes which now gazed at her with an unaccustomed interest.

" Then he is a fool," Dudley said, " for this evening there is not one amongst the Queen's ladies to compare with you. In a tight-sheathed bud it is a puzzle to discern the beauty of the flower that will be, but when the petals start to open, then one knows. . . ."

He was drawing her to him, and a wild panic caught at Morag. She had hated him for so long, had yearned to avenge Amy's heartbreak, yet now she was not wholly repelled. With an effort she broke away from him, aware that her cheeks were hot. " If Her Grace asks for me, then I must not keep her waiting," she said, and went before him into the lighted room.

Dudley, who well knew the physical effect he had on most women, smiled secretly as he followed her. It was true that she had flowered, and, since but recently she had been such a thin, colourless wisp of a girl, that intrigued him. Amy, he recalled, had said that she would be a beauty one day, but he had scoffed at her as he often had, for Amy had said many foolish things. He had never understood her, or wanted to, though he had married the pretty heiress willingly enough. There had been nothing in Amy's personality to hold him, and her childlessness had been a bitter disappointment. To her also, no doubt, poor woman, he thought, and she had endeavoured to compensate by taking this girl and treating her, if not as her own child, at least as a dearly loved young sister. It was likely that she had often bemoaned her sad fate to Morag, who had not attempted to conceal her dislike of him and her resentment. This had mattered nothing, and had only lightly glanced across his consciousness, but now, with the lanky, pallid chit so transformed, there might be some amusement in overcoming it.

Dudley wondered if Guy Erskine was deeply smitten. If so, since the lad had served him well, he might hesitate to compete with him, but he had a shrewd suspicion that Guy's taste was for a more buxom, coarser type of beauty. Morag, as she stood by the Queen's side, looked ethereal: a delicate dryad of a girl, with her fawn-coloured hair, cream skin and the jewel-green of her long eyes.

The Queen was displaying the waxen models of her

hands, which were now set forth in a glass case. Although this was ostensibly to praise Morag's work, her main object was to call attention to the perfection of her own long fingers and delicately formed wrists. The ambassador had sufficient wisdom to praise their beauty more than Morag's modelling, though when the Queen said that she was now urging the girl to try her skill at sculpture, and had had some thought of sending her abroad to work under the famous Van Eyton, he agreed that it might be worth while to give her the opportunity. Smiling at Morag, to whom Elizabeth had referred as her ward, he said that this must surely commend itself to her ambition, and paid graceful tribute to the Queen as a royal patron of the arts.

"I should but disappoint Your Grace," said Morag.

"Why so? It seems that I have more faith in you than you have in yourself."

"I do not think," said Morag, "that I should have any aptitude for—for chipping marble or stone or even wood. I am only confident or content when handling wax or clay. Sculpture must be quite different. And besides," she added as the Queen frowned, "I should be homesick and heartbroken to be so far from Your Grace."

Elizabeth, though she might be chary of loving individuals, yet desired individual love more than most people. She took it with greed. It had seemed ridiculous, even to herself, that she who was given so much adoration should yet secretly have resented Morag's faithful devotion to the dead Amy Dudley; but so it was, and now it gratified her that at last the girl's love was transferred to herself.

"We shall see," she said. "I would not have you unhappy, child, for there has been too much grief in your life. There is no such great haste, and we will speak more of this before coming to a decision."

Morag was dismissed, but those who had not seen the models of the Queen's hands now crowded round to gaze upon them and to make their comments. Robert Dudley said they could have been the hands of two separate women —a queen and a saint. The hands with glittering rings upon the fingers, threading a long, gold chain, were, if anything, less beautiful than the hands folded in prayer. It was so also with the Queen herself. Those who had the privilege to see her in simple, unadorned garb could witness that the translucent beauty of her skin shed its own radiance.

This was on a par with many of the fulsome compliments which could never be too extravagant for Elizabeth's taste, and only she knew that Dudley's tribute concealed something more personal, more private.

That morning, waking early, she had thrown open her bedroom window, and the sun had poured down on her. Dudley, slowly riding his horse, had passed beneath. He had gazed up at her, doffing his plumed bonnet in salute. She had stood there in her thin white bedgown, smiling down at him, and kissing the tips of her fingers to him.

Afterwards, when he had passed onwards, she had gone as any lesser woman might to her mirror—one of the rare Venetian mirrors, costly and beautiful, that had lately replaced the steel or copper reflectors with which her own mother had been content—to convince herself that she truly was as alluring as his ardent gaze had proclaimed. Though in critical mood, she could find no fault with her slender shape, her white skin and the cloud of fiery hair. And then with hand circling her long, slim neck, she had thought of how in Mary's reign she had feared to have it severed from her body, and had remembered her mother's words —heartbreakingly courageous. It should not be difficult for the swordsman sent from France, Anne Boleyn had said, for she had a very little neck.

Shivering, sick with pity and rage, as she still could be when she thought of her luckless mother's fate, she had turned from the mirror, and the fair day had darkened for her. But this evening it was radiant, and presently she was asking a distinguished visitor if Mary—her sister in Scotland —played the virginals with exceptional skill, and whether she danced with surpassing grace.

Tactfully she was assured that although the Scots Queen was passable at both, she fell far short of Elizabeth's grace and proficiency. At this she glowed, as any happy girl might have glowed, exulting in the knowledge that there were still many years of youth ahead of her. But even when she was no longer young, she would still be beautiful, she secretly vowed; or at least her people would believe her to be. Her mother, though swarthy of skin, with little actual loveliness except her long, slanting eyes and her wealth of black hair, could, when she chose, so 'twas said, bewitch all men with the belief that she was flawless, and had gone to her brave death radiating such enchantment that even the executioner had stayed his sword, waiting for her to compose herself, to kneel, to pray, and with her poor, marred hand give the signal for the flashing sword to descend. Anne had been thirty-three, and she had passed through much grief and shame and tribulation, but on that death morning, she could have been a girl of eighteen, stepping forth to meet her bridegroom. Had she known in a moment of premonition that the child she had borne would one day be England's most splendid queen, and subservient to no jealous tyrant of a husband? Perhaps she knew now, and was triumphant.

Dudley was not the only one who caught that flash of exultation, that conscious majesty, which gave her an added allure. He knew the mood in which she could be aloof and proud and not for any man, for all the occasional softening of her heart. His own sank. Though still her favourite, he was only within rigid limits her lover, and often doubted if he would be more.

Kate Ashley, reporting as was her custom, even the most minor incidents and unsubstantiated trifles that came to her notice or her ears, duly informed the Queen that she had reason to believe Guy Erskine had set his covetous eye on Morag.

"I would not blame the maid," she said with a show of fairness, "for she is not one to draw a gallant on with her becks and her smiles; but he has hung around her of late, coming upon her while she is at work and making much of her. There has not been a deal of that up until now, for she had not the looks to make the men a danger to her. But she has changed, Your Grace."

"As most maids do, at her age, Ashley. 'Tis but nature working in her, and soon her mind will be fixed on marriage. Guy Erskine might do as well as another. What is there to be said against him?"

"Naught that I know of, Your Grace, save that he is said to have dallied with more than one of these silly, giggling girls whose duty it is to attend on Your Grace and to be of some comfort to you."

Elizabeth retorted dryly: "Truly, that should be their duty as you say, but you know well that parents petition for an appointment at court for their daughters, in the hope of marrying them off to a rich and titled suitor they would scarce meet in country manor houses. 'Tis a trial for me as their mistress, since should such marriages turn out ill, I am covertly held to blame for it. That is why I refuse to countenance nuptials unless the girl is old enough and sensible enough to make a wise choice. Better to send her home, the lovesick little fool, and then what transpires is not my responsibility. 'Tis different, however, in the case of one of the Queen's wards, as Morag is, and if necessary I will take steps to deal with this matter."

Elizabeth was more disturbed than she would allow her old governess to suspect. She did not want to part with Morag, or not yet a while, though she had a liking for Guy Erskine, and did not forget that she owed him gratitude. He had been a loyal, daring youth, and she was aware of his present discontent. Sooner or later, with or without her permission, he would leave the country and take service in the armed forces of some other nation—unless there should be trouble with Scotland or Ireland, or war with France, which God forbid. Elizabeth was a realist and saw no glory or excitement in war of any kind, but men, as she resignedly accepted, were different. Unless their time was taken up with improving their estates, for the benefit of their families, especially their sons, they were in constant need of occupation. Even Dudley, who rarely left her side for any length of time, would welcome one of the insurrections constantly threatening in Ireland. He would demand to be in command of the troops sent to quell it. In imagination she could see the fiery glitter in his eye, and his ill-concealed glee, though he would be leaving her, and, as in all such forays, would run the risk of being wounded or killed. Elizabeth sighed, and then she smiled. This was what men would ever be, and none could change them.

After this, although she said nothing to Morag, she watched her narrowly, divining a change in her. The girl might well be in love as Ashley had hinted, and when this was so, with one who was favoured by her, it was always to her discontent. Overnight a gay, amusing companion, interested in the feminine pursuits which were not unimportant to the Queen, would become absent and moody, dreaming over her embroidery, caring nothing for the riding and hunting in the great park which made Windsor the Queen's favourite residence, and with no mind for the masques and pageants that enlivened the long autumn and winter months.

Speculation as to how far Morag was involved with Guy Erskine was cut short by a domestic calamity. The dreaded sweating sickness broke out again that autumn, and penetrated to the country districts. There was an outbreak near Hatfield, where Elizabeth had spent so much of her youth, and where Guy's home was situated. Both his parents fell ill, and were dead within a few hours of each other. The distressed Guy was given permission to absent himself indefinitely. Elizabeth felt a natural pity for the young man, who had been grey-faced with grief and worry when he had told her of this sudden tragedy. Morag was shocked and full of sympathy, for Guy had been fond of both his parents.

"And now it's to be supposed we shall see far less of him," said the Queen, curious as to Morag's reactions. "He will be missed, but we can scarce expect him to neglect all else for the sake of his position here, minor as it is. He was an only son, and Linkfields has been the family estate for generations. It will behove Master Guy to marry and settle down and beget a family—the dull fate which in the end overtakes most of the dashing gallants."

Morag soberly agreed. Guy, she knew, was attached to his country home. He had often spoken of it. The old, silvery-grey house, battlemented like a castle, dating from Plantagenet days, rejuvenated some fifty years ago, when it had been given twisted chimneys and a great hall with a vaulted roof had been added. The gardens and dairy had been his mother's pride. The horses, bred by his father, a fine breed, had sold for high prices, and so had the other livestock.

Guy had presented Linkfields in its most roseate light, trying to inflame Morag's interest and putting forth broad hints that he could not delay much longer before choosing a suitable bride. But that his father was competent to manage the estate, and had a remarkably efficient land steward, he would have felt it his duty, Guy had said, to live there, but as it was, there was no such inducement. "My sire," said Guy "insists that I am too much of a swash-buckler to make a good landlord."

As the weeks passed, further disquieting news reached Morag. Guy wrote to her in an unhappy vein. His father,

45

it appeared, had, during the last year of his life, run into difficulties. The horse-breeding, which had been a major activity, had of late been run at a loss; debts had been contracted, and were still owing; and the vaunted, trusted land agent had proved to be a rogue, lining his own pockets at the expense of his employer. When exposure was inevitable, the wretched fellow, wrote Guy, had blown out his brains with his own pistol. Now it was probable that Linkfields would have to be sold, and he—Guy—a homeless wanderer, would seek his fortune abroad.

Brooding with dismay over this letter, Morag looked up to find Lord Robert Dudley watching her from the doorway. Her heart gave a nervous flutter. He glanced at the paper in her hand and said: "You have had tidings from Linkfields?"

"You know what has happened . . . the new trouble that has come upon Guy?"

"Aye. He's in a bad way, poor lad, and deserves sympathy. None of what has come about is through any fault of his. His father was a stubborn fellow and would take advice from no man. There were those who warned him against Pencast, the agent, a smooth-spoken varlet. I did so myself, having heard divers stories of his expenditure, and the lavish fashion in which he lived, but 'twas a waste of breath, and old Erskine set his face against Guy learning how to run the estate. Jealous of his heir, which is no uncommon thing with fathers."

"Guy talks of selling Linkfields and living abroad," said Morag in a troubled voice.

"In which case, mistress, you might never see him again. Is't that which draws such worry lines across your brow?"

"I was thinking of Guy, my lord, not of myself."

Dudley gazed at her searchingly. He picked up from the table the puppet which was completed and costumed, save for the short cape upon which she was now working. "'Tis a good enough semblance of Guy, and a clever piece of work. The Queen shows her good judgement when she says you should be taught to carve or sculpt."

Morag shrugged. "None seem to think that my own inclination is of any importance."

"The inclination of maids is apt to change quicker than the weather, though it is true we have had a settled spell for the last fortnight. Come riding with me in the park, Morag."

She shook her head. " I cannot ride. Her Grace said I was to have lessons, but the most I can do, and that clumsily, is to sit an old palfrey that has but the energy to amble. I have no skill for sports such as hunting or shooting or archery."

" You dance with much grace, however. So did Amy. . . . I remember her at our wedding feast. She was beautiful and admired by all. We were thought to be a fortunate pair with a fair future before us."

Dudley would have found it impossible to say why his lips were so suddenly unsealed, unless it was through an irritated determination to fix Morag's attention on him. " We were in love," he went on, " but were both too young to pledge ourselves for a lifetime of fidelity. Amy's fidelity to me did not waver, but she had few temptations. In the beginning our separation was not of my choosing, and she was loyal to me; visiting me when I was imprisoned. . . . It was an ill chance . . ."

He broke off, but with unexpected boldness, Morag finished the sentence for him: " That the Queen was lodged in the Tower at the same time."

" We survived it the better for each other. You should have seen her in those days, child. She was—unforgettable. To-day she is magnificent—strange, subtle, enchanting; but then, she had the dew on her. She was in fear of her life, wondering each day if it would be her last, accused of conspiracies which she had not so much as heard of; but her courage was a thing to wonder at. Each day, that bullying Gardiner was there to question her, to accuse her, to set all his wits against hers, to trap her. But she was too swift for him . . . she did not utter one incautious word. Me, she learnt to trust, though we feared to speak to each other above a whisper. . . ." Dudley ended with a sigh.

So that was when he had first learnt to love Elizabeth. Morag was conscious of a heart-forgiving understanding. Who *could* have resisted that gallant royal girl in all the pathos of her youth? Dudley saw the new gentleness steal over her. " Amy," he said, " never condemned me as you have. I would she could have been happy without me. I gave her all that was in my power to give; freedom in her

47

restlessness . . . she could travel the country as she listed. She had jewels, all the fine clothes she fancied . . . she had you. More, I could not give her."

Morag said nothing. The sheets of Guy's letter had fallen to the floor, and she stooped to pick them up.

"You have a fondness for that lad?"

Morag bowed her head. "A fondness, yes."

"Not love as maids think of love? But in sooth there is more between you than there oft is at marriages arranged for a mutual advantage."

"*What* mutual advantage, my lord?"

"There may be such. Amy, with my good will, left provision for you. Did you know of it?"

"I heard—not long ago."

"You could, perchance, help to mend his fortunes if the Queen so wills. Sooner or later she will be constrained by her conscience to make a match for you. She is slow to do so, but she owes something to Guy Erskine."

"She does not owe *me* to him!" cried Morag in alarm.

He laughed. "One would think I was set to sacrifice you to a monster. It is a goodly lad. Never fear but that he would be kind to you . . . as who would not?"

On an impulse he drew her up from her chair and into his arms.

"My lord!" Morag protested, but the hardness of his body was against her softness, and she felt resistance seeping out of her. "I had ceased to hate. I pray you do not make me hate afresh," she entreated.

The words rang out with such a desperation of sincerity that Dudley in astonishment released her. Neither of them had given a thought to the half-open door, or were aware of the shadowy figure that for an instant stood there and then passed on.

FIVE

The Queen concerned herself over Guy Erskine's ill fortune. He had not himself acquainted her with it; for this she perhaps liked him the better; but she questioned Morag, and was shown the two letters that Guy had written to her. Elizabeth gave the matter thought.

It was possible that she owed Guy her life. As a mere stripling he had acted on Dudley's orders, but he could have refused to run such risks; he could have bungled, or even betrayed them. The relationship between Elizabeth and Mary, then on the throne, had been curious and painful. Unscrupulous ministers and priests had endeavoured to make pawns of them both, poisoning the mind of the elder sister against the younger, and driving fear and resentment into Elizabeth's proud heart; yet through it all, Mary, to whom Anne Boleyn on the eve of her execution had sent a message of entreaty to be kind to her helpless babe, had never lost her love for the half-sister whom as a child she had protected. Nor had Elizabeth forgotten that in those past days Mary had been the dispenser of bounty—the grown-up sister who not only had replenished her scanty wardrobe out of her own meagre funds, but had played battledore and shuttlecock, and hide-and-go-seek in the gardens of Hunsden and Hampton Court. It had seemed incredible that Mary should believe her a traitor, but she had been jealously conscious of Elizabeth's popularity with the people, jealous of her youth, angry because she refused to profess herself a Catholic. Mary could be goaded to extremes by anger, and had Elizabeth not been exceedingly cautious, she would certainly have come to a violent end.

Even with such caution there had been traps and pitfalls hard to recognise. From at least three of these, Guy, obeying Dudley's instructions, had saved her; perhaps not so much through love of her as through the excitement of adventure. "Nevertheless," said the Queen to Dudley, "his reward is long overdue."

"I doubt not he considers himself rewarded by your graciousness to him," Dudley replied.

The Queen glanced at him sideways with mockery, and her laugh rang out. "I would I could believe in such selfless devotion. Service not only deserves reward, but it is expected—land, money, titles, advancement. If I delayed to reward Guy Erskine it was because when I was proclaimed Queen, this was a poorer country than it is now—a feeble fleet and army, and empty coffers. But now I will do all I can for him. Write to him, Rob, in my name, and command him to be at Westminster next week, when the court moves there."

"Am I to give him an inkling as to this reward?"

Again there was the flash of the Queen's mocking mirth. "How canst, since I have not consulted with you, nor come to a certain decision? Nay, say no word to him, Rob, though I will talk it over with you. Think you that a marriage should be brought about between him and Morag Trevenna?"

The question shot out quick as light, and Dudley's mental antennae quivered warningly. He was convinced that even a few days previously it had been Elizabeth's intention that Morag should not wed for years. Not only was she averse to youthful marriages, but she had a genuine fondness for the girl, and was interested in her potentialities. Her attitude towards Guy Erskine was less certain. She smiled upon him, as upon all the attractive young men with court positions, but it did not follow that she was blind to their faults and weaknesses. There was no mystery about Guy's. He had few if any intellectual interests, was vain of his looks and of the ease with which he attracted women. As against this, he was brave, loyal to his Queen, devoid of grasping ambition. He was an accomplished lute-player and possessed an attractive tenor voice.

Dudley did not believe that a few weeks ago Elizabeth would have considered him as a husband for Morag. Her choice, had the girl shown a yearning for marriage, would have fallen on one older and more stable. Dudley, though he had jestingly recommended Guy to Morag as a possible husband, felt a twist of the heart, as he contemplated the sacrifice of such artless innocence to a licentious young philanderer. But he knew better than to show it. Could it be possible that Elizabeth suspected how strongly the girl's swift change from scrawny childhood to lovely womanhood had moved him?

"It is your right to be consulted," Elizabeth said. "For nigh on two years she has been the Queen's ward, but before then she was, being your wife's cousin, under her protection, and since she was dowered with your permission, you have some responsibility for her. Tell me, would you commend this marriage?"

"With a man who is now nigh penniless? Morag's dower, though generous, is not sufficient to mend his broken fortunes."

"Nay, but 'twill be of help. For the rest, I will do such as is necessary; sufficient gold to buy fresh stock, refund what that villain agent stole and squandered—perchance a knighthood. It could be the beginning of a new prosperity, if Guy has the will and steadfastness to settle as a landlord, which should not be difficult with a young and lovely wife."

Dudley said: "'Tis a rich reward, Bess. More than he could have hoped for or expected."

"Oh, as to that, it is his necessity that decides the reward. Less would be of little service to him. But I would hear from your own lips, since you know him well, that he is worthy of Morag."

"There is not much harm in him," said Dudley, convinced now because of the cool, assessing gaze fixed on him, of under-currents. He did not dare suggest that some lesser maid should be selected for Guy. Elizabeth's suspicions, which could be only nebulous, would flare into a certainty if he protested.

"And what of good is there in him?" she persisted.

"Bess, you can read a man's heart and mind better than most. I doubt not he will gladly wed her, and with a knighthood, and his fortunes repaired, 'tis not a bad match for her. He will treat her well, I trow, seeing she is so high in your favour."

"That will assure her little. Once wed and living in the country, we are not like to see much of Morag."

The royal "we," which the Queen so rarely used when they spoke privately, and the coldness of her voice, were danger signals, but whatever Dudley's faults he was no coward, and he said boldly: "Methinks you are of a mind to rid yourself of the girl—that she has become redundant."

"Mayhap she has . . . mayhap I am growing old and would not be reminded that it is ten years and more since I was as fresh as she."

"But you . . . are you! Are you crazed, Bess, so to compare yourself?" He seized her hand and kissed it.

Elizabeth softened. "Oh Robin, would I could be sure of you."

"Of whom could you be more sure?"

She was silent, having come to a decision, to which through pride and subtlety she would adhere. Dudley might suspect that she knew of his fancy for Morag, but he would never be certain, for she would not accuse him. When she had passed that carelessly half-open door, it had seemed to

Elizabeth as though history repeated itself. So had Katherine Parr, dearly loved stepmother, stood and watched her in the arms of Thomas Seymour, Katherine's husband. Younger than Morag, Elizabeth had yielded to him, kindled to him, only vaguely understanding the life he had aroused in her. Though her stepmother must have fathomed Seymour's perfidy, she had behaved with splendid dignity, reproaching neither of them. But in order to preserve the fragile structure of her marriage, as well as for Elizabeth's own sake, she had sent the girl away. They had never seen each other again, for Katherine had died in child-bed. One could take a lesson from Katherine, the Queen reflected. There would be no reproaches, but Morag should be removed from temptation, with no hardship for her in this decision. She had shown a liking for Guy Erskine, and it was natural, after all, for a maid to marry. Her dowry would be put to good use, and Guy's fortunes would be repaired. Both might be considered fortunate.

"Why *won't* you marry me?" Dudley demanded wrathfully. "Secretly, if need be."

"And how long, think you, would it remain secret?"

"As long as you so willed, though there seems scant reason for secrecy. Whatever the unmerited suspicions cast on me at the time of Amy's death, that has passed. An heir to the throne is so much desired that the father of the child would be tolerated, whosoever he might be."

How lightly men spoke of child-bearing, reflected the Queen with rancour. To listen to them one might imagine that it was no more of an agony than to have an aching tooth drawn, though in truth that was pain enough. They blandly ignored the danger of producing progeny, though it was far from uncommon for a lovely, blooming girl, marrying with joy, to be dead before a year was out. She thought shudderingly of Jane Seymour's death—of Katherine Parr's—of several others'. There *were* those who bred easily, but not such as she with her narrow hips and her delicate physique. Sometimes she acknowledged that this horror of child-bearing had become an obsession, but nevertheless the sex antagonism had never been stronger, as she said:

"If I marry, it will be in my own good time, and I shall marry as a Queen, of my own will, not as a weak woman goaded into consent because such is thought to be fitting. Never will any mortal being coerce me, and do not you, Robin, forget that I have said so."

Pale and sobered, Guy waited upon the Queen. The court was now at Westminster, and she received him in one of the smaller privy chambers. He was dejected and nearly penniless. No one had prepared him for the honour of the accolade, and he could scarcely believe it as the sword fell lightly on his shoulder and the words were spoken which conferred a knighthood upon him.

The Queen enjoyed giving surprises, and could when it pleased her be astonishingly informal. She was informal now, as she indicated with a gracious motion of her hand that Guy should seat himself. She grieved for his bereavement, she told him, not only from compassion, but because she had personally esteemed his mother. She had heard of his financial losses.

"Perhaps more freely than you would have been prepared to tell me, and you must not blame your sweetheart because she showed me your letters. That was by my command."

"My sweetheart, Your Grace?"

"Surely she must be called such, though you have been discreet and loyal, knowing her to be our ward. I trow, however, that you are worthy of Morag and will do well by her."

Guy listened in near-stupefaction as she swept on. His future, he perceived, was already mapped out for him, and doubtless he should be thankful that it was so little disagreeable to him. As a boy and a young man he had served the Queen faithfully, and now the reward was great. His father's debts would be paid, the family coffer filled, and Morag's dowry would be at his disposal. Though the Queen would be loth to lose him from court, she considered that his duties to his ancestral estate should be his first preoccupation. It would take all the years of his young manhood to build it up as one would build up and fortify a small kingdom. Morag was young, but the Queen was confident that she would make a worthy wife for him.

Resolved to override any possible objection Guy might make, until she had said all she intended to say, Elizabeth gave him no opportunity to interject a word, even one of gratitude. The wedding should not be delayed, she told him, and she as the bride's guardian would be responsible for all the expenses attendant on it.

When she at last ceased to speak, Guy, half-stunned, could only thank her with, he declared, the most feeble inadequacy for the title she had bestowed upon him, and for her wholly unexpected generosity. As for Morag, it was true he had an affection for her, but he had no certainty it was returned.

"Of that she shall herself assure you," the Queen said, and one of the attendants clustering at the farther end of the chamber was sent to fetch Morag.

She had been prepared, though only within the last few hours. Elizabeth sending for her had in the most casual way spoken of her fondness for Guy. She had airily assumed that it existed, had not questioned it, but had delivered an ultimatum. It was time Morag married, and it was her will that Guy should be her husband. She would have a title, a delightful country home, and a young, charming and devoted husband. What girl could ask for more?

Listening to her, Morag realised that no protests would avail. When the Queen issued a definite command there could be no disobedience. She guessed that there must be some secret reason for this imperious decision, but did not connect Dudley with it. What was a casual embrace to such as he? And how should the Queen know of it? Morag's own instinctive response to Amy's husband, whom she had convinced herself that she hated, was a greater trouble to her.

Now she knelt before the Queen and was smiled upon. "Here is your lover, who has suffered much and is in need of your loving consolation," Elizabeth said.

They were left together, and at first no words were spoken. Morag's head drooped, her gaze was fixed upon her hands folded in her lap. Guy admitted that she was fair enough, and recalled that the thought of marrying her had crossed his mind. But it had been but a vague thought, and he had scarcely believed that though they might be deep in love, the Queen would give her to him.

And now, without entreaty, she had.

Guy's glance roved over her. Her fair hair was partly hidden beneath a gold mesh cap, but the sapphire velvet dress outlined her graceful young body. She was pale and nervous, at which Guy could not wonder, guessing that this marriage command had been sprung on her with as little ceremony as it had been sprung on him.

"This should be a happy day," he said at last, tentatively.

"For you, perchance. I heard—Her Grace told me this morn—that she would confer a knighthood on you, and that your fortunes would be mended, as a reward for risking your life on her behalf when she was but the Lady Elizabeth."

She spoke with spirit, and Guy asked: "Will it be so odious to marry me?"

"No—but I would we had been allowed to make our own choice."

"Sweeting, you *are* my choice. My heart was set on you, and with the Queen's permission or not, 'twould have been told, but for the sickness that carried off my parents, though from my letters you could have guessed. To whom else did I write, bleating out my misery?"

"I thought naught of it, but that we were in sympathy."

"'Twas more, Morag—much more. Dear heart, can you not bring yourself to love me?"

She sighed. "I—I hope so, Guy. My mind is adrift, for I am troubled by a strangeness in the Queen. She has oft said she could not part with me, or not for many a long year."

"And now you are wounded because she parts so lightly?"

"Yes."

"But Linkfields is not so many miles from London. You can still be at court from time to time."

"I do not think she will want to see me at court," Morag said soberly. "'Tis as though this marriage she commands is a banishment."

"How so? She spoke of you to me with fondness, and as though she gave us both our heart's desire. To set me up again will be to dip deep into her privy purse, and there is my knighthood to boot."

"Her Grace owed you as much, but not—but not—she did not owe me to you."

"Sweet, you speak as though you are a serf, to be sold at the Queen's will."

"Is it so very different? How dare I disobey? What would be my fate if I did?"

55

"She could not send you to the Tower for it."

"Well—no . . . and perchance I exaggerate, but I am sure she would no longer keep me about her person as her favoured ward. It mystifies me that she has so changed her plans. For the Twelfth Night revels there was to have been this puppet show—a pageant of puppetry, she named it. I should have been hard put to it to have fashioned the many puppets needed. There was to be a theatre built, a showman—this you know, but each time until these last days when she spoke of it, there was detail added. She was set on it, and then she changed. 'Twas as though it no longer interested her, and now 'twill be all thrust aside. Long ere Twelfth Night, I shall be married and at Linkfields."

Guy made light of this. Women, he thought, were driven by their whims. "Some other plan has engaged her fancy," he said.

He looked upon Morag with a strong desire, for which her reluctance was responsible. Most maids in her anomalous position would be elated at the prospect of such a marriage. He had had a fondness for her, but no more; but now it might be more, for all that there was Rose Yarrow in the background of his life, a full-blown, experienced beauty, well versed in love.

That Rose was crude and vulgar mattered nothing to Guy. He could not have married her. He knew he was not her first lover and would not be her last, but she was what he wanted and he would not discard her for any marriage, though for a time he might have to show consideration for his bride, which he would do, he told himself, intrigued by Morag's coolness and by the anticipated pleasure of breaking it down. She would, as she matured, make a worthy chatelaine for Linkfields. His mother would have approved of her.

Drawing Morag into his arms, Guy was conscious of her fragility. He kissed her, coaxing a response from her. There was a certain pleasure in it, though he knew himself to be a lazy lover. There was no necessity to woo Rose Yarrow, save by gifts he could ill afford. Her earthy passion was his at a touch, though it might not be evoked for him alone. But she took reasonable care not to arouse his jealousy, and if he installed her at Linkfields as housekeeper, he could keep her in order.

His mother, who had known that the girl was his mistress

and kept by him, had grieved over it, but had been helpless
to break up the affair, though Rose, who had been employed
at Linkfields, had been dismissed, suffering some local ostracism in consequence. She would expect him to make this
up to her now that Linkfields was his, and she would be
none too pleased when he brought home a wife, whom
she would have to serve with respect. But Rose would make
the best of it, Guy reflected. There would be new dresses
for her, and the gaudy trinkets she coveted—the thick gold
chain for which she had pestered him, the dangling earrings—
and the fact that she would be set above the other servants
and in control of them would do much to appease her.

SIX

By the Queen's orders the wedding was to be a grand
one. There would be a feast to follow it, and Kate Ashley
was told to see that the future Lady Erskine was suitably
equipped. It was to take place at Windsor, though the court
was not usually in residence there at this time of year. But
Windsor had been home to Morag since Amy Dudley's
death, and often when the court removed to London she had
been left behind there with her tutors and a suitable duenna.
Elizabeth had wished to preserve the childlike aloofness which
from the first had pleased her, though she had known it could
not be preserved for ever.

But now that Morag had shown herself to be as accessible
as other maids, and might, if not married and settled in the
country, even become a rival, the Queen's aim was to remove
her as soon as possible from the temptation of Dudley's
renowned fascination. But this should be achieved with all
honour, even with a pomp that might be thought excessive
for a girl whose court position had never been clearly de-
fined.

Elizabeth, adroit as she was in evasive tactics, took care
to see as little as possible of Morag. There was the one
formal interview when she gave the affianced pair her bless-
ing, and another on the eve of the wedding, when with her
own hands she fastened a triple string of pearls about the
bride's neck. In the few weeks before then, Morag had
little time to brood. There were constant fittings for the

new clothes, which were of a grandeur to awe her. It seemed to her that as the wife of a country squire, even though he had been elevated to a knighthood, she would have little occasion to wear half of the elaborate gowns, though as country houses were notoriously cold and draughty, she might well be glad of the fur-lined wraps and the quilted cloaks.

Guy assiduously paid court to her, and succeeded in breaking down much of her shyness. She was not in love with him, but he had persuaded her it was so with him, and in her loneliness and bewilderment she drew warmth from his caressing fondness and was grateful for it. Most of her personal possessions, to which the Queen added several items, were sent down by carrier to Linkfields, and Guy took himself off there thrice, with the explanation that their private apartments were undergoing alterations needing his supervision. The Queen had given a fine suite of French furniture for the bridal chamber, a most welcome gift, Guy said, for his parents had had the same furniture for the thirty years of their marriage, and it was old and battered, and could now be removed to the attics. He bought a fine four-poster bed, hung about with azure-blue brocade curtains threaded with silver.

The Queen with a selection of courtiers and ladies returned to Windsor for the wedding ceremony, which took place in one of the large audience chambers.

Morag felt as one might who was swept along on a strong current. It was hopeless to try to resist it. She had every reason to be grateful to the Queen, and so had Guy, whose reckless, boyish chivalry had rewarded him so well; and yet she was ever more persistently aware that the Queen had closed her heart to her, as definitely as her long fingers might have closed a book upon a chapter she had read.

On her wedding eve, with the Queen's pearls about her neck, Morag escaped from the many who had clustered around her of late, praising the wedding gifts, envying her her gay, attractive betrothed. Wrapped about in her cloak, she slipped out upon the terrace. It was a cold, fine night, with a full moon riding in the sky that seemed to be more darkly blue than black. The moon silvered the grass, and the bare boughs of the trees; those delicate spreading branches were, thought Morag, more beautiful in their skeleton state than when thick with foliage. She

58

wondered, rather sadly, if she would ever see Windsor again. Perhaps—but not, she guessed, for years, and then only rarely. Now that she was leaving it, she felt an aching love for the beautiful old castle, for the grounds and the noble park. She had been miserable when first brought here, but she had learnt how to be happy, and for that the Queen was largely responsible. Yet she had hated Elizabeth, and had told herself fiercely that she would always hate her, when she had first been interrogated by her. She, in conjunction with Robert Dudley, should have had a curse work on them, if Morag had had her way. But now, with a curious wistfulness for the single-hearted child she had been not so long ago, she knew that she had lost the power to hate. She was awed by the Queen and admired her, and had been swayed by a half-acknowledged fascination for Dudley.

In their one unexpectedly emotional encounter, he had stirred her, as Guy, to whose allowed caresses she was now becoming accustomed, never had. These she accepted dutifully, but had she followed the impulse of her pounding heart when Dudley took her into his arms, she would have been a sorrier maid than she was to-day.

Two years previously, had it been predicted that she would grow up to be sufficiently fair to catch Dudley's fancy, she would have seen the ensnaring of him as a dramatic, double vengeance. How clear the vignette would have been had such a possibility occurred to her. A pretended surrender, and then Dudley's faithlessness betrayed to the outraged Queen, who in her fury might have sent Dudley to the Tower, and would certainly have banished Morag. She could in her mind's vision, see the small, clear picture as though this debacle had actually come about.

Instead, she had not given a thought to the beloved Amy, though she had despised herself for her weakness, and had set up such a rigidity that the astonished Dudley had perforce set her free, when in her heart she had not wished to be free.

She sighed, so heavily that it seemed as though the faint whisper of a rising wind echoed it, and then there came the irate voice of Kate Ashley.

"For a half-hour past I have searched for you. What do you here in the dark and cold by yourself? And you to be wed to-morrow! You should be abed by now. Her

Majesty asked for you; she had a mind to speak to you privily."

"But she has already given me audience—and these," Morag said, touching the shining pearls about her throat.

"Aye. I knew of her intention, but this was something else it seemeth. Belike some eve-of-wedding counsel that she deemed necessary. But now 'tis too late . . . one of Her Grace's sick headaches has been threatening throughout the day, and the toothache besides. She has endeavoured to fight it off, in vain."

"Can I not see her, then?" asked Morag, as Mrs. Ashley took her by the arm and propelled her towards the side door through which she had escaped.

"You cannot indeed. The revels were cut short, Her Grace being too dizzy to sit upright. She has gone to her bed, poor love, and I have made her a posset of powdered marigold leaves which will help to relieve the pain. She never thinks to spare herself," said Mrs. Ashley aggrieved, "and this grand wedding of yours is but another tax on her."

"I did not ask it or expect it," Morag retorted with spirit. "If I must be married, a quiet wedding with only a few witnesses would suffice."

"Such ingratitude!" Kate Ashley drew in her breath with a sharp hiss.

"I am far from ungrateful, that is why before I sleep to-night, I would fain see the Queen to tell her . . ."

"Nonsense, child, she is already drowsy, and I wot you thanked her when she gave you the pearls."

"Yes . . . but . . ."

"Then get you to your bed, or come to-morrow you will be a pale and heavy-eyed bride, when to please Her Grace you must be in full beauty. I vow that white and gold kirtle is a dream. . . ." Thus chattering, Mrs. Ashley energetically propelled Morag to her own room, where for once she waited on her as a maid might—brushing her long hair, sponging her face and hands, and tucking the bedclothes round her. Morag suffered all in silence. The impulse to confide in the Queen had swayed her. Ever since Amy Dudley's death her lips had been closed upon a secret, but this evening with the sense of all life changing, the past slipping rapidly away from her, she had suddenly had the wish for candour.

60

She would have told Elizabeth, had Elizabeth been available, and in telling she might still alter a royal destiny. But now, none might approach the sleeping Queen. Kate Ashley would not countenance it, and there was the armed guard before the door.

A great weariness passed over Morag. She could do no more, and what she could tell might have less significance than she had, as a child, supposed.

The mellow beauty of Linkfields was at least no disappointment.

Morag, after a month of marriage, thus sought to console herself. Nominally at least, she was now mistress of this large, rambling manor house, stone-built, with its squat turrets and twisting chimneys. Morag thought it as beautiful in its humbler way as Hampton Court. There were terraced gardens leading down to a wide stream, and beyond it acres of arable land where cattle grazed, and a park where the deer were plentiful. Within the house there was comfort as well as beauty: exquisite oriel windows, graceful arches, high, carved ceilings, panelled walls.

As a bride, exhausted by the festivities, even before starting on the journey from Windsor, she had uttered a gasp of admiration when she had entered the great hall on her husband's arm. The hall was large and square, with a vaulted roof, and a stone floor strewn with fine rugs. A graceful staircase, elaborately carved, led from it to the first floor, which circled the hall as a balcony. On the ground floor there were large living-rooms, and a door which led to the kitchen quarters. All the rooms were pleasant, with wide casement windows, well-polished furniture, deep stone fireplaces in which log fires glowed.

The servants were drawn up within the hall to greet her, headed by a fine, buxom young woman who spread out stiff, silk skirts as she curtsied to the new Lady Erskine. She, Guy told Morag, was Rose Yarrow, the housekeeper. All the servants were newly engaged, for half a score or more had died of the same sweating sickness that had carried off the master and mistress of Linkfields. The others had fled in terror from the old house with its dead or dying occupants, deeming in their superstition that a curse had fallen upon it. But that was all over. Every particle of the house, the outbuildings, the dairy, had been fumigated. Guy himself had superintended these operations, and it was now more than four months since the last case of the deadly illness had been reported in the neighbourhood. The epidemic had passed.

In the first dazed hours, Morag had asked few questions; nor had she made criticisms, though she had been struck by the general youth of the inside staff. She had hoped for an elderly, or at the least a middle-aged, housekeeper —somebody with a semblance of Mrs. Ashley's fussy motherliness. Rose Yarrow was handsome, and probably capable, but she was no more than twenty-seven or eight, and Morag, from the first, had felt a vague discomfort when the bright brown eyes had scanned her inquisitively.

Of all the fine rooms at Linkfields, Morag least liked the big bedroom with its great canopied bed and the French furniture that had been the Queen's gift. But she might, she admitted privately, have felt differently had the consummation of their marriage been a happy memory.

A month later, having somewhat recovered from the shock of being so roughly possessed, she tried to make excuses for herself as well as for Guy. It could not be that one alone was to blame. She had been frightened, fatally ignorant, and alas, far from real love, though in her loneliness and sense of strangeness she could have been wooed to loving, had Guy possessed sufficient tenderness and consideration. He had shown neither, though for that there might be some excuse through the quantity of liquor he had taken. Shudderingly, Morag recalled an impatient roughness nigh to brutality. Of fondness there had been little, only the urge to conquer and possess, and she, though unresisting, had been unable to respond with any degree of ardour. Not only physically hurt, but repelled, spiritually shattered by his assault, she had wept for hours after Guy had fallen into a drunken stupor, and then there had been the anticlimax of the early morning when he had awakened with a crashing headache and was violently sick.

Once this was spent, she had done what she could for him, pouring cold water from the ewer, sponging his face, and drying it on her own fine towel, coaxing him to fall into a more natural sleep than that which had kept him tossing and turning the night long. But when on his recovery he had reached for her again, she had pushed him away, for which she doubted if he had yet forgiven her, even though

62

on subsequent occasions, when he was sober, she had submitted as a good wife should.

Now, with the marriage a month old, it was surprising how little she saw of Guy. Fortunately he was bent on becoming a good landlord, and also fortunately had taken a fancy to the new steward, a man somewhat older than himself, who had been recommended to him by Sir Richard Adrian, his nearest neighbour: a bookish stodge, according to Guy, but rich and successful.

Though Guy's father had fallen out with him, Sir Richard had ignored the feud when mortal sickness broke out at Linkfields and had proffered all possible help. He and his wife had done all that good neighbours could do, and finally, when the master and mistress lay dead, with several of their domestics, he had insisted that Guy should stay with them until he was in a fit state to put his affairs in order. When the extent of the financial disaster was discovered, Sir Richard had offered a loan, which Guy might have accepted but for the Queen's bounty.

He, who had never been encouraged by his father to interest himself in the estate, had much to learn, and Stiles, the land agent, was an able instructor. Sir Richard had gone to some trouble to procure the man, who was acting as under-steward to a landowner in a different county and was eager for a position of more responsibility. Stiles's parents were Sir Richard's farmer tenants, and Guy was assured he could trust the man.

Although expressing gratitude to Sir Richard, it was a resentful gratitude, partly occasioned because it was impossible to cut a swaggering figure when all knew of his father's folly and the poverty to which he would have been reduced but for the Queen. It was also shrewdly surmised that Morag had not come to him empty-handed. Guy realised with secret wrath that she was already pitied because of his association with Rose Yarrow, which was common knowledge. This, since Rose was no innocent, and was older than he and the seducer rather than the seduced, would have been tolerantly overlooked, but for his hardihood in engaging her as his housekeeper—a cruel insult to his innocent bride.

Guy, though not particularly concerned for Morag's susceptibilities, saw no reason why she should suspect that the girl was his mistress, and as she was no adoring bride, he appreciated Rose the more, and persuaded himself that she would be discreet and civil. Without a doubt Rose was capable. She had a good-humoured way of exacting work and obedience from the servants under her, and the cook now employed at Linkfields was a crony—a coarse, middle-aged woman who thought it a good joke that the new Lady Erskine—poor, whey-faced scrap of a thing—had no idea that Rose was their master's doxy. To Mrs. Stiggs, Morag's tentative effort at friendly co-operation was a cause for ribald laughter. As for Rose, she despised Morag, and yet was furiously jealous of her.

The Adrians had already proffered hospitality. Guy and Morag had dined with them a few evenings past, and Morag had liked the grave Sir Richard and his much younger wife who was London born and bred and, as she said, had had difficulty in adapting herself to a country life. But that was all over. She had been married for eight years, and had two small sons. It was plain to be seen that she dearly loved her quiet husband, and Quince Hall, their well-ordered home.

To Morag she had been warmly kind, not putting on matronly airs though she was seven or eight years her senior. They must be friends, Erica Adrian said. It was a splendid thing for her that there was a new, young mistress at Linkfields. The other country houses were all at some distance, but Quince Hall was only separated by a few hundred acres.

Afterwards, Guy had grumbled. It had been a dull evening. There had been no long lingering over wine with Sir Richard and Erica's brother, who was staying with them recovering from a toss he had taken from his horse which had resulted in a broken leg. One of the most famous London surgeons had set it, but it had been long in re-knitting, and Stephen Clinton still limped slightly, and used a stick when he walked for any distance.

Morag had scarcely spoken to him, but had thought that he looked interesting—a tall, slenderly-built man in his thirties, with a thin, beardless face and thick chestnut hair. Guy had declared him to be a dotard—nothing to say for himself—and of all the outlandish things, a playwright. "Weighing everyone up, in order to use them in one of his plays, I make no doubt," he said.

Morag wanted to know if the plays had been produced, and

Guy said grudgingly that they had; at one of the London playhouses. To Morag this was extremely exciting. There was so much in this strange new life that could have been exciting and delightful, had her personal life been happy. But already she doubted if that could ever be, and not solely because she had married Guy at the Queen's behest.

There *had* been a fondness, and with time, given a greater kindness, it might have ripened; but now fondness seemed to have drifted away.

She did not believe Guy greatly wished to make love to her, and for herself she dreaded it. He made his demands upon her with a dogged persistence, determined to exact what he considered his due. Already he had reproached her for coldness, for being so little a woman that she did not welcome a husband's embraces. The night before, they had had their first real quarrel.

"If I'm cold, 'tis no wonder," Morag had flared. "Ignorant though I am of love, methinks you have little for me, else you would be gentle, kind, and . . . and talk to me, explain to me . . ."

"Explain what?" Guy had laughed scoffingly. "What's there to explain in mating, which comes naturally, even to the brutes in the fields."

"But we are not that, and I cannot believe that every girl who weds, finds it so little to her liking."

"Well, there you are right, but most women, heaven be praised, have warmth. You should have taken your dowry to a convent, rather than have so deceived me."

"Deceived you? How?"

"With those sidelong looks of yours. You were all agog to be married, and it's my belief you talked Her Grace into speeding it on. For what other reason would she have been so quick to part with you?"

"I know not why, but it was not because she thought me eager to wed. That I was not, but I had no choice, and nor had you, since it was her wish."

"Mayhap 'tis not too high a price to pay for Linkfields. Do your part. Give me a brace of sons as soon as may be, and then I'll trouble you no more."

If Guy expected tears or clinging or reproaches, he was disappointed. Morag said not a word, nor did she try to keep him, when with a curse he flung himself out of bed and their room. Sure that he would not return to it that night, she sighed with relief. Nor did she wonder where he spent the hours until early morning, when from the window she saw him tearing across the fields on his favourite horse. There was more than one bedroom ready for occupation, and he had the choice of them.

But although angered and shocked by his treatment, she was also a little sorry for him. He, as well as she, had been pressed into this marriage. It was true he had fleetingly dallied with her in time gone by, but he could not have had any serious intent. Even had the Queen overlooked defiance of her stated wish, how could Guy have resisted it, after the munificence of her generosity?

To Morag the future was in many respects bleak, but unknowingly Guy had opened a window for her. If he desired an heir or heirs, she also desired children, and would give them a wealth of love. She could, she thought, be a good mother, even though she might be inadequate as a wife, and the sooner she was with child and rid of Guy's marital attentions, the better. She was too innocent, too ignorant of a man's nature, to reflect on his sexual deprivation. Besides which, she instinctively divined that there was no ardour in his rough, cursory handling, and vaguely supposed that his possession of Linkfields satisfied him.

She believed it could also satisfy her. She could devote herself to learning all there was to be learnt of household lore, and when she held an infant in her arms . . .

Her spirit rose on a tide of hope and longing.

SEVEN

Although Erica Adrian was an able horsewoman and Morag a most indifferent one, the two fell into the way of taking a daily ride together. Erica, in order to pacify her thwarted horse, would sometimes canter on ahead and return to Morag ambling along on the fat, lazy mare that the Queen with a jesting remark had given her before her marriage. As she said, the creature had become accustomed to Morag, and might die of the shock did any other rider attempt to make her briskly trot.

" 'Tis a true proof of your friendship," said Sir Richard

dryly, "that you are willing to accommodate yourself to that poor girl."

Erica shook her head denyingly. "I enjoy her company, and as a general rule I have the time to exercise Jupiter before calling at Linkfields for her, and by then he is less lively. To be seated on a beast of any kind has the sense of perilous adventure for Morag, and I doubt 'twill ever be otherwise. I suggested this morning that it might be more agreeable to her to take coach drives, in ours for preference since it has been newly sprung; theirs is in a poor state, and as Sir Guy never uses it, it is to be supposed he will be in no hurry to acquire another."

"His expenditure must be heavy, having bought new stock and settled so many debts," said Sir Richard. "Whatever our personal opinion of him, he seems to be settling down to his duties as a landowner."

"Well, yes, and 'twas not his fault that he knew nothing when he inherited. He is fortunate to have Thomas Stiles for guidance."

"Fortunate in more ways than he deserves," remarked Stephen Clinton, "though mayhap he did do the Queen some service. None great enough, however, for the gift of a wife in addition to all else."

Erica glanced at her brother in some surprise. Usually Stephen was tolerant to a fault, but now there was a biting note in his voice, and his brows were drawn together in a frown. It had been a chilly spring day, which had ended with a downpour of rain, and now after the evening meal the three of them were clustered about a heartening log fire in what was known as the oak room by reason of its panelled walls and polished floor. It was a pleasant room, as were all the rooms at Quince Hall. Red damask curtains were drawn across the windows; there were screens worked in tapestry by Erica to nullify possible draughts; a settle and high-backed chairs were cushioned for comfort, and a massive draw-table was usually littered with books and papers.

It amused Erica somewhat that although a room had been set aside in which Stephen could work on his new play, and her husband might have been expected to do the work connected with the estate in his office adjoining the gunroom, and she herself had a boudoir, stylish with the French furniture now so much admired, nevertheless they had all fallen into the habit of collecting in the oak room, when there were no guests to necessitate the use of the big drawing-room.

Sir Richard now sat at the table with his account books before him; Stephen, with his left leg, still apt to tire, propped on a stool, had a book of plays on his knee, and she had brought her tapestry-work which was never-ending. Chairs, curtains, screens, all bore witness to her skill and industry, and were more beautiful than even she imagined, fond though she was of designing flowers and formal landscapes to be copied in jewel-coloured silks.

The three of them, she reflected, were extraordinarily companionable. They preferred to be together, even if they scarcely uttered a word for an hour or more. She wished that Stephen could stay at Quince Hall for ever, and once he was over the pain of his injured leg, had been glad that the excuse of it had brought him to the country, where she could give him some attention, and more comfort than he would have in his London house, where he had none to wait on him except two elderly servants, who had no notion of doing anything more than was an absolute obligation. Yet she knew that it was unlikely she could persuade Stephen to stay throughout the summer. He loved London, which eight years ago Erica had been glad to leave, and which she now chiefly remembered as a place of disagreeable smells, hustling and much noise—vastly unhealthy, she was sure, though Stephen for all his spareness of build never ailed, and last autumn's outbreak of the sweating sickness had demonstrated that those who lived in country parts were not immune from epidemic dangers.

Stephen's small house was wedged in a narrow street near the river and the theatre where three of his comedies had already been shown with some success. Had he been penniless he could scarcely have earned a livelihood with his playwriting, but fortunately he was not dependent on his work. Their father had been a prosperous city silk merchant, and had left his son and daughter with ample means. Both their parents had died some years ago, soon after Erica's marriage. It was surprising that Stephen had not also married, for although quiet and inclined to be dreamy, he was extremely attractive—more than one girl had openly shown that she found him so—yet so far as his sister knew there was nobody of serious interest in his life.

"One supposes it was by Morag's own will that she married," Erica said. "Why should she otherwise, since she had a pleasant and privileged position at the Queen's court?"

"Are there truly pleasant positions at court?" Sir Richard asked sceptically. "You could have had one yourself, my love, but you declined it."

"Because I was married, and had two young children. How could I bear to leave you all for the regulation months of being in waiting? Her Majesty understood, and it has always been my belief that she did but offer me the honour as a formality: knowing I should beg to be excused from it, but deeming it my due, because when she was at Hatfield, secluded, and as the Lady Elizabeth in disfavour with Queen Mary, we were able to show her a few kindnesses. Her Grace has a great capacity for gratitude, and rarely forgets those who have tried to serve her."

"'Tis true, and her generosity to Erskine is but another proof of it. I would there were not this evil gossip concerning him. Erskine, when in his cups, and that is not infrequent, has no still tongue. Much to Dr. Rice's disapproval he has seen fit to take notice of his eldest, who has but just served his time at St. Thomas's Hospital and has returned here to assist his father. 'Tis a clever lad, but of some wildness, and one cannot wonder that this friendship brought about by Erskine has aroused the good leech's apprehensions—the more so as the lad is loth to settle down in the country. Elated at such notice, Peregrine Rice has boasted at the village tavern, and has been heard to join with Erskine in slighting talk of Morag. 'The pill in the jam' was Erskine's description—and he went on to tell young Rice that the Queen made the taking of her as a wife a condition of her setting him on his feet."

"The wonder is," said Stephen, "that there was not one amongst those who listened, prepared to use his fists in disgust at an insult to a gentle lady."

"They scarce could, since it was an overheard conversation," Sir Richard pointed out. "Erskine lowers himself by spending so much of his time at the tavern; not that he has much standing. He can be as lunatic haughty as overfamiliar with the yokels, depending on his mood and the amount of liquor he has taken. Moreover, gossip also concerns itself with the wanton he has seen fit to set up as housekeeper at Linkfields. Has Morag any suspicion of her, think you, Erica?"

"I am sure she has none, and she would be the last to hear of the insult and wrong to her. Even an enemy, did she possess an enemy, would wish to spare her. One can only hope Sir Guy will tire of the slut and get rid of her, before betrayed by some trivial carelessness. Nevertheless," and Erica sighed, "it is plain that she is not happy."

"How should she be, with that graceless lout as spouse?" asked Stephen.

"Oh, as to that, his manner is sufficient pleasing. He almost, if not quite, conceals that he finds us intolerably tedious. He is good-looking also, and able with the lute, besides having a fine tenor voice. He would need to have some such qualities for the Queen to have suffered him at court."

"If no more than superficial, 'tis surprising he won the heart of a girl not only lovely but intelligent."

"I wonder if he did," mused Erica. "Morag utters no disparaging word, but it strikes as unnatural when one so newly wed rarely mentions her husband. There may be something in the story that they were both pressed into marrying."

Sir Richard said with some austerity: "My love, we are now falling into the village gossip. 'Tis no concern of ours what brought about the marriage."

"It becomes a concern if one is fond of Morag—and I *am* fond of her. There is that about her which is childish and defenceless and calls forth the impulse to protect. Sir Guy will be away for the next week or more. Lord Dudley is to journey to the north on some mission for Her Majesty, and he invited Sir Guy to accompany him. Morag thought it natural enough, seeing that he was once Dudley's page and accustomed to travel with him. It crossed my mind that she might be lonely at Linkfields, and I asked her to stay with us during his absence. Sir Guy, when asked, was agreeable, and I hope you have no objection, Richard. She is not like to be an obtrusive house-guest."

"You know well that you are at liberty to ask anyone you choose to stay here." Sir Richard's gaze rested affectionately upon his wife. "It was a good thought of yours in this case. One would be hardened indeed to be without qualms thinking of the poor girl left alone with none but

70

the Yarrow jade and the other servants at Linkfields, several of them not of the best repute."

"I only wish," said Erica, "that Sir Guy had enlisted my help when engaging an entire new household. 'Twould have been a natural action, since he turned to us for help when his parents died. But—foolishly—he set this duty upon Rose Yarrow. She has brought in her own friends and relations, who regard her, not Morag, as their mistress. It could become almost intolerable for her."

"She has the right to dismiss the entire pack of them, if she chooses," Sir Richard pointed out.

"Wives have no rights, if denied a husband's permission to order their household as they would. Only one older and more experienced than Morag would dare to take such a drastic step, and even so would need a good excuse. I do not imagine that she has the excuse of openly uncivil treatment. Yarrow appears to be capable. All was orderly, and the dinner well served and cooked, when we dined at Linkfields."

Stephen said: "Her personal waiting-woman should surely be of her own choosing."

"As yet she has none, but 'tis odd you should speak of it, for only yesterday she said she had one in mind, and had the intention of bringing her to Linkfields. 'Tis a girl who was in the service of Lady Dudley. She was at Cumnor at the time of the accident. Morag liked her and has written to her occasionally, and this girl—Joan Brownstone is her name—is discontent in her present situation. Sir Guy has already told Morag that it is fitting for her to have such an attendant; I surmise because the uppish Yarrow objects to be called upon for any extra service, and although he may have expected the choice to be Yarrow's, Morag has sent to this girl offering her the situation. She is expected any day, and Sir Guy though he may be disconcerted at such choice can scarcely berate Morag for it."

"For one so young, whom we rightly or wrongly suspect of suffering coercion, that is a bold move," Sir Richard observed. "Does Erskine as yet know nothing of it?"

"We—ell no, he doesn't." Erica's expression, though tinged with guilt, was smug, and her husband's eyes twinkled with an amused comprehension.

"I trow she will keep quiet about it at your suggestion."

"I did say, passingly, that the appointing of this maid

71

appeared to be a matter for Morag alone, and that although her husband might think it meet to give employment locally, he would not send the girl away once she was installed at Linkfields."

Both men laughed outright. "Sister, you have a gift for diplomacy," said Stephen.

"A kindly name for craftiness, but I was justified, Stephen, or so I considered."

"Indeed you were. I applaud you, and speaking for myself am rejoiced that the poor girl will have about her one who has some regard for her. From what you say she may sorely need it."

"At the least," Sir Richard said, "we can do our best to make her visit here a cheerful one."

"The children will see to that, dearest. Morag has a way with her, and they both love her. She invents stories for them out of her own imagining, and she makes the most astonishing lifelike little models in clay to illustrate them. They now have a complete farmyard with chicks and geese and doves and lambs and cows. Morag says 'tis the first time she has attempted to model animals, though she has a gift for making figurines and even modelled the Queen's hands in wax. There was talk, it seems, of sending her to Holland to study with some famed sculptor there. 'Twas a pity, perhaps, that this scheme came to naught."

"A thousand pities," Stephen agreed.

But he was not wholly sincere, though for Morag's sake he could have wished she had been spirited away to foreign parts before the Queen had decided to marry her to Guy Erskine. For his own part, he knew already that his meeting with Morag, though as yet they had but exchanged a few words, was momentous. From the instant that his gaze had alighted on her, his life had changed. There had been that leap of the heart, that quickening of the pulses, which although it was a new experience to him, he had recognised as a sign of strong attraction. She was different from any girl he had ever met—but he had dreamed of such a girl —a fragile dryad, slender and beautiful, with such beauty as might be passed over by those who looked for bright colouring and buxom charms. To him she was exquisite with her long eyes of changing hue and her fawn-coloured hair. Her shyness enchanted him, and her smile was all the more ravishing because it was infrequent.

Now he scarcely knew whether to be glad or sorry that for a week or more they would be under the same roof. He had an urgent wish to know her better, but doubted the wisdom of it. Naught could alter the fact that she was married. If he became seriously enamoured of her, it would be to his certain pain. Not possibly to hers, though a girl unhappy in her marriage, as it seemed Morag must be, was, however virtuous, in the state too long for consolation.

Stephen did not visualise himself as a conqueror of female hearts. Although not ill-looking, he had no gift for easy fascination, and was inept at paying compliments. He could write plays, but not verses praising the length of some beauty's eyelashes, or the swan-like turn of her neck. He was no lute-player or songster, possessed none of the facile charm or talents that would have graced Elizabeth's court. This he did not regret, and even now, though so urged to make sympathetic contact with Morag, he thought it as well for safety's sake that he was no polished courtier.

Later that day, as he passed along the upper hall, he saw through an open doorway that two maids were preparing a guest-room. One, taking in an armful of lavender-scented sheets, started to spread them upon the bed; the other was hanging fresh curtains at the window. Such preparations could be only for Morag. He could picture her in that pleasant, sunny room, peacefully asleep, her long fair hair spread on the pillow, her hand beneath her cheek.

A lover's fancy. He recognised it as such.

Morag said: "I cannot think of anything that is more interesting than the writing of plays."

"Might not the writing of books be more so?" Stephen asked.

She shook her head. "Not to me. On the stage, characters are brought to life as never in a book."

"But first it is necessary for the play to be accepted and produced."

"There is the same hazard in writing a book—it must needs find a publisher who will have it printed and distributed."

"All the arts are a hazard," Stephen agreed. "There is no certainty of selling wares, as in a mercer's business. But 'tis true it's a heart-stirring occasion when a character of one's own creation takes life from those who portray it.

Yet sometimes—too often—it's not such life as one had imagined, and always, to me, the female characters lack reality, since by convention boys must needs enact the parts."

"But you can scarce tell the difference," Morag argued. "I have seen several plays given at court, and should have been deceiving into thinking the boy actors were women, only that I knew it was not so. They are trained from childhood, are they not?"

"They are, and many are gifted, yet in my eyes they fail. This masquerading is a fashion that will pass, and I can but hope in my own age. 'Tis a common complaint of playwrights that it stultifies their inspiration. Not that I would make so bold as to say I am inspired. I have some natural turn for writing, but I am no heaven-sent genius."

Morag said candidly: "That I cannot judge, as to my sorrow I have not seen your plays, and now, as like as not, I never shall."

"Why so? Surely you will visit London from time to time? In the late autumn a new play of mine is to be shown at The Curtain. Richard and Erica are bound to visit London to view it, and would bring you with them."

"That would be wondrous kind. . . . It would be exciting, but I doubt my husband would give permission."

"An you coax him, he will likely take you himself to visit your friends, and then an evening at the play is a commonplace."

"I made very few friends," Morag said. "For the great part of the two years that I was the Queen's ward I was kept to my books. I met none as young as myself, and those older had their own affairs to occupy them. It was only in the last months that Her Grace allowed me to attend the court balls. She said once that she would keep me a child as long as she could. That was no tyranny, for I was willing. In childhood there is peace—and privacy. I was in no haste to be a woman."

"If this was the Queen's humour, why such willingness to let you marry young and leave her protection?" Stephen asked bluntly.

Morag, who had often wondered the same, shook her head dumbly. She had been playing with the children in the garden when Stephen joined them, and soon after, Erica had come down to the bowling green where Stephen was

74

giving the two boys instruction, and had taken both off for a ride. Now Morag and Stephen sat together on a rustic seat, and she dreamily watched the play of a little fountain which cascaded over a group of stone dolphins. The grounds at Quince Hall were even larger and more elaborate than those at Linkfields, and Morag had not yet fully explored them. She said:

"In the little wood here, the bluebells were half-open three days ago, and should be in full bloom by now. I love them above all spring flowers, but there seem to be none at Linkfields. Last year I picked an armful at Windsor and filled my own rooms with them, begging jars and bowls from the pantries."

"From a single root they will soon spread prodigiously. Before you go home I will dig some for you, though happily you won't be leaving for a few days."

"No." Morag perceptibly brightened. "My husband, on leaving, thought he would scarce return until next Monday or Tuesday. It is a very heaven here. Erica is gay and content, and the children are dears—fun to be with. I have more taste for company than I supposed. . . . Sir Richard's and Erica's friends are kind. When a party of them rode over yesterday they were all merry and very friendly to me. I wish . . ." She broke off and said, resolutely dismissing wistfulness: "The sky is clouding over. I would fain see the bluebells with the sun upon them."

"Must you be alone to enjoy the sight of them?" Stephen asked as she rose and moved away.

"No—I—no, but I remembered your leg, and Erica's anxiety that you should not over-exert it."

"I would say rather, that exercise is beneficial, and we can take the short cut through the yew alley." As he fell in at her side, he gazed searchingly at her half-averted face and asked: "What should the end of your 'I wish' sentence have been?"

"Oh, just a grumble. I seem to be much given to grumbling these days and should be ashamed. I did but think how pleasant 'twould be to have visitors—friendly and informal—coming and going at Linkfields, as they do here. But none have called on us."

Nor would they, Stephen reflected pityingly, for there was too much local scandal over Rose Yarrow's presence at Linkfields. Neighbouring squires might overlook it, but their wives refused to. Guy Erskine would have to dismiss the girl, to show regret for his profligate ways, before pardon was extended to him. Most of the families of consequence were Protestant and puritanically inclined, and as Guy's father had been morose and quarrelsome, a great trial to his more agreeable wife, who had perforce to fall in with his ways, there were no old friends sufficiently tolerant to turn a blind eye upon Guy's misdeeds. Sir Richard had shown excessive charity in his dealings with the son of an old enemy.

" 'Tis early days as yet," Stephen said, striving to comfort. "Few of those who live within visiting distance had met your husband before he inherited Linkfields. He was taken up by my Lord Dudley whilst still only a lad, and rarely here, so I'm told, save for brief visits. It must be allowed, I fear, that his father was a curmudgeon who made himself uncommonly disliked."

"But that was not Guy's fault," said Morag. "His father treated him ill, and he was chafed because he was denied all responsibility. When that dreadful plague carried off so many at Linkfields, one might have expected sympathy and kindness, but none showed it save Sir Richard and Erica."

"The majority were in mortal fear of the infection," Stephen said. "All families thus inflicted were apt to be shunned."

"Except by those at Quince Hall. How good they were when Guy most needed it. Yet Erica must nave had fear for the little boys, as well as for Sir Richard and herself."

"They were sent away—to Rutland, where we have a small colony of relations. Have patience. Now that the Savilles and the Altons have met you here, and have been, so one and all told Erica, much taken with your sweet ways and looks, you may be sure there will be a difference in their attitude," said Stephen, hoping for this against his better judgement.

"Sweet ways and looks!" Morag was genuinely surprised. "But I am said to be gauche and cold-mannered."

"Who says so?"

"We-ell . . ." She broke off in confusion, unable to say that she was repeating Guy's critical remarks, which were frequent. " 'Tis true, I fear. I *am* awkward and apt to be

76

tongue-tied, though not with you, who are so kind you put me at my ease."

"That is a sweet thing to hear."

"But 'tis not through coldness. The reverse is true. I find it easy to become fond—but that through shyness, does not show."

They had reached the little wood by now, and having made her naïve admission, Morag fell silent. The sun filtered through the pale green leaves of the trees upon a carpet of azure blue. Not even at Windsor had she seen anything quite so beautiful. Stephen, though also sensible of the beauty of the scene, gave more attention to her rapt face. Her eyes shone, her smile was a child's smile of ecstasy: "Nothing in heaven or upon earth could be more lovely," she said. "I wish—I wish I could stay here for ever —or at least I wish they need never fade."

"The memory need not fade, Morag."

"It will not." She saw that he had coloured as though with confusion and said: "Sir Richard and Erica call me Morag, so why not you? I find it difficult, after all these months to answer to Lady Erskine, and surely between friends 'tis needless to be formal."

"Then let me hear you say Stephen."

"I have thought of you as Stephen from the first," she said simply.

He took her hand, and held it for a moment before he raised it to his lips. She smiled at him, and he said: "Friendship—your friendship would be a precious gift."

"It is yours. Few have thought it worth the asking, though I could be a good friend, I think."

It was only a fraction of what Stephen wanted from her, but it must suffice. In his heart he honoured her as much as he loved her, and although as yet he knew little about her, there were times when he felt as though he knew all; as though in a silent communion between them, there were no secrets. She was gentle, intelligent, loyal and tender-hearted, and sorely unappreciated by the man who should have cared for her above all others. Stephen suspected that she was not only neglected and unconsciously insulted by Rose Yarrow's presence, but treated with positive unkindness.

But that was something he dared not dwell upon, for the

anger which rose up in him. So far as was possible, he would ignore Guy Erskine's existence.

"There is naught in which you should hesitate to command me," he said quietly. "All I have, and all I am, is at your service."

Intuition told Morag that it was more than a flamboyant compliment. Her eyes widened, and she paled slightly, as involuntarily she glanced at the hand he had held and kissed. It was as though that ceremonious salute, no less than his last words, were a pledge.

"I know not how to thank you for such friendship. 'Tis more than I merit, but I—I shall treasure it," she faltered.

"You will not forget what I have said?"

"Never. How could I? Nobody before has ever said as much. 'Tis as though we both lived in King Arthur's times, when his knights made such vows."

"Many very ordinary men have made them since, and women, mayhap, have been comforted by them."

"You . . . you comfort me," Morag acknowledged in a whisper, and so doing, confessed her need of comfort. Much more was said without words as Stephen's gaze held hers. Turning slightly away from him, she said with an effort at lightness: "'Tis a shame to disturb this glorious blue carpet, but if a few flowers are picked carefully, perchance it will not show."

"Hundreds could be picked without notice"—and Stephen started with strong, deft fingers to break the tall, green stems. Morag watched him. There was a sense of unreality upon her, but a happiness struggling through, such as she had never known, even in the days when Amy Dudley had loved her. This was love also—but of a different kind, and although a man's love, there was no fear in it or danger. Stephen was to be trusted—absolutely. Stephen was to be believed, though why he should choose to love her, she could not imagine.

"You want these to decorate your bedchamber?" he asked.

"Not only mine. The little room leading from it is to be used by my maid. She is on her way here, and will arrive before I return to Linkfields. Erica and I walked over there yesterday, and I gave orders that Joan, when she came, was to be directed to Quince Hall, with such of her baggage as would suffice for a few days. She is travelling by carrier, and it is uncertain how long the journey will take, but 'twill be to-morrow by my reckoning, and flowers in a room are a welcome, are they not?"

"You must be fond of the girl," Stephen said.

"Oh yes . . . she was good to me when I was only an unhappy child. I was sore-hearted to part with her when I was taken from Cumnor to Windsor. 'Tis selfishness to be glad she has not married, and so is free to come to me now, for most girls wish for a home and a man and children of their own; but Joan wrote that she could not be happier than to be with me, and Erica was sure that Guy would not object, even though the housekeeper was . . . well, almost insolent, saying the engaging of servants was her business, not mine. Erica overheard, and reproved her for it."

"Not half as sharply as the wench deserved, I'll be bound," Stephen said. "For myself, I am thankful you will have this young woman to wait on you."

They strolled back towards the house, Morag carefully carrying the great sheaf of bluebells across her arm. Stephen thought that were he an artist he would paint her so, in her full-skirted gown of a delicate shade of pink, and the great splash of blue, and the sun on her light hair.

As they neared the terrace, a servant hastened towards them. Behind him there followed a tall girl in a neat dark travelling dress, with a broad-brimmed, high-crowned hat, fastened with ribbons beneath her chin. Morag gave a glad cry and ran towards them, and some of the bluebells fell to the grass as she caught Joan Brownstone's hands in hers.

"Oh, how happy I am to see you!" she cried; and then she laughed shakily, because Joan, mindful of her manners, and of Morag's now elevated station in life, bobbed a curtsy. "Oh, Joan!" She leant forward and kissed the older girl on the cheek.

From a short distance, Stephen watched with approval, relief, and a smile for Morag's unconventionality. His keen gaze was a summing-up. Joan Brownstone, neat, inconspicuous, with firm features and a pleasant smile, was Rose Yarrow's antithesis. Her affection for Morag was evident. So far as lay in her power, this new waiting-woman would take care of her, Stephen decided.

EIGHT

"'Tis a lowering to me that you rate this of so little importance." Rose Yarrow's voice shrilled in anger. "When you asked me to oversee for your ninny wife who knew nothing of the ordering of a household, 'twas a bargain 'twixt us that I should have free choice to give employment where I listed, and when you left to join my Lord Dudley, you knew nothing of your wife's sly plan to bring this Brownstone here as her waiting-woman. It angered me, but I said naught, for I could not, my Lady Adrian being in hearing when I heard Brownstone was to be her personal attendant and would be high above all save myself. I doubted not that you, when you returned, would send Brownstone about her business, but I might have known that, weakling as you are, you would give in to her."

The tirade had lasted for over twenty minutes by the timepiece, and Guy, at first prepared to coax and reason, had at last been brought to an anger that was rare where Rose was concerned, but the greater because she had no care to lower her voice or consider that her fellow servants might be within earshot. In the midst of her harangue he had pulled the curtain from the door, to find that it was ajar. There had been a quick scuttle of footsteps and the flash of skirts disappearing down the passage. Had Rose intended her loud reproaches to be overheard, as a proof of her power over him? That would have been in keeping with her insolent arrogance which did but increase with every week.

Guy, in his turn, now felt resentment. He had sacrificed the esteem of those who were his social equals because of Rose, and there were times when he was humiliated by his ostracism. Yet she gave not a thought to this, or if she did, she held it of no account.

"You go too far," he said. "Silence your tongue, ere you say that which will force me to cast you out."

Her big brown eyes stared at him incredulously, for he had ever been at pains to conciliate her. She flung back her head and laughed. "'Twould be half a day at the most 'fore you were after me, begging me to return, and that I

80

would not, for I oft weary of serving your tallow-faced wife. There are those—there is one in particular who plagues me to wed him, and 'tis a temptation to give him the answer he craves."

"You settle in the village as a labourer's wife—to live as a peasant and scrub and cook and spread each groat to do the work of three, as against all you wheedle out of me? A likely tale!" But although Guy scoffed, his face had reddened in jealous anger.

"'Tis no labourer, but Giles Tipper the journeyman. 'Twould be a life to suit me, travelling the country and seeing all the sights. Tipper does a good trade and is a likely fellow."

"Has he had you?" Guy demanded bluntly.

"Nay. I keep my side of the bargain, if you do not. I swore to keep faith while I lived here, and you swore she was a nothing. A half-wit moppet, pressed on you by the Queen, who knew not what else to do with her."

"I swore no such thing. 'Twas you who put your own meaning on the little I said, which was no more than that 'twas not a love match on either side. Did I not insist that as my wife she must be treated with respect?"

"Aye—for public show, and respect she's had, though all despise her. She had not the spirit of a mouse until my Lady Adrian took up with her, and I make no doubt spurred her on to send for this Brownstone, who looks down her long nose at all of us and coddles her as she might a pampered child."

"Your mistress has known her for many a year."

Rose flashed at him: "Do not dare to call her my mistress when we are alone. 'Tis I who are true mistress here, as all the stiff-necked gentry know, and keep away because of it, as though the place is accursed."

"If the women-folk in general do, that suits you well, who would think yourself demeaned to wait upon your betters."

"My betters!" Rose flung towards the door in a fury, and might then and there have been as good as her word, departing to find new excitement and flattery elsewhere, but that Guy intercepted her.

Reason told him that he would be the better off without her. She did but prey upon him. She had lowered his prestige and probably cared little for him. But although in

81

looks she was coarsening, the spell still held, for as a mistress she satisfied him. Now, catching her by the arm, he pulled her into his embrace, laughing with pleasure when she fought him. He kissed her roughly and repeatedly, and presently she no longer resisted him, and they sank down together on the settle. Rose wept a little then, protesting that he treated her so ill it was a marvel she put up with it, but finally she returned his kisses, and Guy took from his pocket a case containing a heavy gold bracelet which he clasped upon one of her plump wrists.

"I bought this for you, and would have given it to you at the first, but that you were in such a rage," he said. "You've badgered me for some such bauble and it cost me a pretty penny. You're an expensive luxury, my wench."

"I'm worth every penny to you." But now Rose's voice was soft, and as she turned the bracelet on her wrist, she nestled to him.

"Not when you act the shrew. My wife means naught to me, as you well know, but I like not to have her bullied. She had no deliberate intent to provoke when she sent for this girl to wait on her. I had told her it was fitting she should have such a one, but she misconstrued, thinking I intended the choice to be hers. When I found this girl already lodged here, I was taken by surprise, but there was naught I could do, for my Lady Adrian was the first to tell me of it, and had high praise for her. Such an old association would bring my wife comfort, she said, and she was sure I would wish her to have comfort. 'Twill mean that you have to do the less for her."

"But I had set my mind on my half-sister Dorcas, but just grown, and fit to be trained as a lady's maid."

"An older waiting-woman is more suitable. Joan Brownstone is near of age to yourself, and already knows her duties. There are times when a young wife needs care."

Rose said sharply: "You mean she is *that* way—already?"

"Not a day too soon. We have been wed nigh on four months. The hope of an heir, and the need for it, was what sweetened this marriage."

Rose was moodily silent. Although she did not love him —was probably incapable of loving anyone—a primitive jealousy stirred. Hitherto it had been a cause for thanksgiving that for all her freedom with several, she had borne no unwanted babes, but the realisation that Guy was now bound to show Morag some kindness and consideration irked her. If she gave him a son, he might even come to prize her. On the other hand, as often as not the mother perished though a babe lived. Rose now nurtured ambitions which even to her would have seemed absurd a half-year ago. Guy was so slave to her charms, that he would, she believed, make her the second Lady Erskine, if death were so obliging as to carry off the first. It was true that the proud county families would never acknowledge her, but there were plenty of her own sort to fawn on her, and men of all ranks could be won over. They wouldn't ignore her, though their wives might.

Hazily, Rose envisaged a satisfactory future. Morag, she reflected, was puny, and with her narrow hips not formed for easy childbirth. Her pale skin and her slenderness were surely signs of delicacy. A word in the midwife's ear might be profitable. There was but one in the village, and although experienced, she was given to drink. When the time came it might be possible . . .

"Well, 'tis only to be expected," Rose said at last, "and 'tis to be hoped she'll have a lusty boy and no puling girl brat."

"God send it," Guy said fervently, "and so you behave yourself, it's you, not her ladyship, who will get a fine present when all is safely over . . . perchance a coral necklace to match the colour in your cheeks, my beauty."

"A ruby on a chain would suit me better," she bargained.

Guy laughed. "So be it. I won't grudge it to you, if you put yourself about to be civil to this Brownstone."

Rose pouted, but said acquiescently: "Of a truth, you always get your way with me."

Erica duly heard of Morag's expectation and rejoiced with her; there was also in her secret thoughts, which she would not utter even to her husband, from whom she kept little, a certain relief. She had much fondness for Morag, but that was not to be compared with her deep sisterly love for her brother. At first astonished, she had after a few days of covert observation become uneasy over Stephen's interest in Morag; an interest which since he was usually politely indifferent to pretty women, she could not discount. Erica had long hoped that Stephen would marry, and Morag would have been most congenial as a sister-in-law had she been single; but since she was married, and moreover unhappily married, the association and the mutual interest were dangerous.

When Morag confided to her, a few days after leaving Quince Hall, that she thought it certain she was in the early stages of pregnancy, Erica embraced her tenderly. "This," she said, "should make a whole world of difference."

"To my husband's esteem for me, you mean? Why yes, I suppose you are right. Should I bear him a fine son he will at least see some useful purpose in our marriage. Until now I have been a sore disappointment to him."

Erica, who thought she had never looked more lovely, sitting in her elegantly-furnished boudoir, with her smooth head bent over the first small garment she was sewing for her expected babe, was lost in wonderment. The veriest boor should surely have been proud of her. Erica strove for the right words, but before they were uttered Morag went on, with a placidity which struck her friend as singular: "But then, so has he been a sore disappointment to me. Mayhap we are neither of us so much to blame as the fate that threw us together. I would not charge it upon Her Majesty. She was led to believe that we had a more than common liking for each other, and indeed I was almost persuaded that I had, and Guy must have been likewise persuaded when he vowed he loved me."

Erica opened her lips and closed them again. She could not and would not tell Morag that Rose Yarrow had been Guy's mistress long before his marriage, nor berate him because instead of paying her off as a more decent man might have done, he had continued the association and had made her his housekeeper. "Dearest," said Erica, "'twould be an easy thing for anyone, man or woman, to love you."

Morag shook her head. "I doubt that an impatient man would find it easy, and Guy has ever been impetuous and dashing and in the need for excitement. I am not exciting, and when we married I was of such ignorance that I think now only an older man of understanding and great gentleness could have suffered me. Love I no longer expect, but ours could still be a seemly marriage. I have a great longing for children, and Guy of an heir. I love your two boys, Erica, and that alone has shown me that with a nursery I could content myself. Oh, I am so much happier, I cannot tell you, especially as there is now dear Joan to be with me. I had some craft," and Morag smiled, " for ere Guy had the opportunity to remonstrate at her being here, I told him I was with child and needed one around who had an old and lasting affection for me. After that, no more was said about it being policy or duty to engage one of the tenants' daughters as my waiting-woman."

" I am thankful you have her," said Erica with truth, and looked kindly upon the tall, neatly-dressed Joan Brownstone when she entered the room with a tray of refreshments for her mistress and her guest.

It amused and touched Erica, as it had also amused Stephen, to observe the affectionate familiarity of Morag's manner to her waiting-woman. From Morag's attitude, Joan could have been a loved relation, though Joan's own attitude was all that was respectful. Erica spoke in friendly manner to her, saying it was a relief to her that Lady Erskine had someone who would watch over her, as only another woman could. This was a pretty part of the country and she hoped Joan would be happy. Sometimes when she called to take Lady Erskine for a coach airing, Joan should accompany them, and if her mistress allowed, Joan would be very welcome at a wedding fête that was to be held shortly at Quince Hall for the head gardener's daughter, who was marrying one of the tenant farmers.

Morag said she would be delighted for Joan to have that treat, and when the girl, after expressing suitable gratitude, had left them, she said: " You are so kind, Erica ; everyone at your home is kind. Your husband and Stephen both made me feel that they were my friends. I know not what I have done to deserve it."

" To be your own self is enough," said Erica.

Morag had uttered Stephen's name in the most natural manner. Her innocence of all guilt was evident, and doubtless such fancy as Stephen had for her would now pass harmlessly. It could be no more than a fancy, engendered by Morag's wistful sweetness. There was so much in her nature as yet undeveloped and for which she had found no expression. She was not naturally weak-natured, but had been suppressed through loneliness and dependence, and few could have a more loving nature. Erica could well imagine the wealth of loving that would be lavished on her child when it was born, and she deliberately said as much to Stephen, when after her visit to Linkfields she spoke to him of Morag.

"'Twill make all the difference in the world to her," she said, "and not a day will pass that I shall not pray for her safe delivery and a fine son. As a general rule I am of the opinion that a small family is the most desirable, and shudder to contemplate the frequent perils that so many wives undergo, with the giving up of all their youth to child-bearing, but for Morag a large family may be her only chance of happiness."

Sir Richard and Stephen had both been present when Erica in a seemingly casual way had said that in the autumn Morag was expecting a baby. Sir Richard had remarked that no doubt Erskine was delighted; Stephen had said nothing, and when Sir Richard was called away to attend to some business, Erica had reverted to the subject, watching Stephen's face, and surprised to see his lips curl in a smile.

"You are pleased about this, for more than one reason," he said. "No doubt a babe will fill a gap in Morag's life, but your thought is that it puts me out of danger."

"Why . . . but . . ." Erica stammered.

"That air of innocence, my sweet sister, is much exaggerated. Let us be open with each other. You were apprehensive when you noted my interest in Morag, and your imagination leaping ahead foresaw catastrophe; perchance an elopement; a duel with her execrable spouse . . . tragedy for the two of us."

"I did not foresee so far as that, only a growing attachment that might cause naught but sorrow."

"It is a sorrow to me already," Stephen admitted, "and that was bound to be, since were I either a wife-stealer or a lecher, Morag would stand fast to her marriage vows, however irksome to her. Half a dozen progeny could not set us farther apart than we are already. It has not entered her innocent head that I love her as a man loves, only that I am uncommon kind of heart. That is how it is, and how it will remain, sister."

"Oh, Stephen, I am sorry," Erica said. "'Tis not as though you are one to have frequent fancies for a pretty face. I fear this has already gone deep with you."

"Aye, so it has, and 'tis no pleasant thought that that churl's seed burgeons within her, but 'twas only to be expected. God grant that all goes well with her. The months of such waiting are long, and I mistrust that ox-eyed strumpet who has Erskine in her toils. She would not baulk at doing Morag some mischief."

"I doubt it, Stephen—she would not dare. Sir Guy with his urgent wish for an heir will have some care for Morag, and now there is Joan Brownstone to guard her. But I wish I had not unthinkingly brought you two together. Of a truth it did not strike me that you would look twice at her."

"Once was enough. With me 'twas that of which poets write, but which before this I have ne'er believed—love at first sight! Don't fret, my dear, perchance this will enrich my life, rather than mar it. 'Twas a stultifying thing after all to be so certain, not that I was incapable of love, but that the one who could arouse it had no existence save in dreams."

"Do you mean that you actually dreamt of Morag?"

"At least of one who much resembled her—of long, greenish eyes and a wealth of soft-coloured hair, and a mouth that smiled tenderly. But mayhap it is a commonplace for those unwed to have some such idea, and in work on the new play, it will be thrust out of mind."

"But you are already working on it, are you not?"

"Haltingly. Strange though it may seem to you, my ideas form more rapidly in the noise and dust and turmoil of the London you now dislike. Gazing from a window at a brick wall is more productive of work than to sit in a fair garden with a shading tree overhead and a paradise of flowers around. These bring about manifold distractions —the breeze stirs the leaves of the trees and they spread a pattern on the paper; the birds sing and the bees hum; the myriad colours of a butterfly rivet the attention; colours blend and blind; petals fall from the flowers. . . ."

Erica said resignedly: "This preamble denotes that you wish to leave us for your city house and your view of a brick wall."

"'Twas understood I should do so when my leg mended, and that it has. My home is in the world of theatres and players. I am grateful to you and Richard who have made me so kindly welcome, but . . ."

87

"Go if you must," said Erica, "though I had hoped you would stay throughout the summer."

"That would not be a good thing, my dear. You and Richard and the boys are enough for each other—complete. Guests, though dear, can become wearisome. But be sure that I shall visit you from time to time."

But not for months; not until he had succeeded in mastering his longing for Morag. If I were not so fond of her, thought Erica, I should blame her and resent her—only for her, he would belike have stayed much longer.

"You will send me word of her, from time to time—let me know how she does?" Stephen asked.

"I promise you."

Justice compelled Erica to admit that Stephen's idealistic love was not Morag's fault. There had been no coy, sidelong glances, no desire to attract. She had not raised a finger to beckon him nearer to her. Fate was responsible for this weakness of love, which Morag probably only vaguely understood. A malign fate had woven Stephen's fancy around a misty dream-girl who bore a likeness to Morag.

Impatience swept sentiment aside. What Stephen needed was not a shadowy dream-maiden but a practical, sensible wife with a sufficient dower, who would make a comfortable home for him, entertain for him, advance his interests. The trouble was that girls who would develop into such satisfactory wives had been available to him for years—had been deliberately put in his path by Erica herself—and they had not attracted him in the slightest degree.

It was too provoking.

NINE

Morag was astonished, and presently, when she searched her mind, almost frightened, because after only a week of Stephen's company she missed him so much. Since Amy's death he was the first person with whom she had been able to talk with complete freedom and enjoyment. He had made her feel that she was understood; her habitual shyness had ebbed away. She knew, not only that she could say anything to him which came into her head, but that it was of interest to him. But although he had succeeded in loosening her tongue, she was equally happy to listen. When he spoke of his plays, especially of the one which he had recently started, it was not only profoundly absorbing, but also flattering. Unaccountably he seemed to think her opinion was worth having, and she ventured to give it. They discussed his characters as though they were real people, and indeed they soon became real to Morag. He told her of his life in London and set up a longing in her to see the little house where he lived, of which he was fond, though Erica thought it shabby and inconvenient, and disliked the narrow street leading down to the river in which it was situated.

Stephen agreed that he could have been better served by the two servants he employed, but said 'twas always so when an unmarried man was the master. The rogues knew they could take advantage when there was no mistress to keep an eye on them.

" You should wed and find one to look to your comfort," Morag had said, and did indeed think that would be the best fate for him. But Stephen, shaking his head, had replied that to be single was far preferable to being unhappily married, and unhappy that state was bound to be, in his view, unless the two people concerned had much fondness for each other. As that was also Morag's conviction, she had not contradicted him.

Stephen knew many of the leading players of the day and could tell amusing, sometimes exciting, stories about them. He described the London playhouses to her, which she had never entered, though she had seen a few plays. When the Queen desired it, actors came to court to perform before her. The description of the free and easy life he led enthralled Morag, but to her he seemed to be more an onlooker than a participant, and when she said so, he agreed. To a great extent, he said, writers were onlookers by nature of their craft, and it was only possible to share one's thoughts with a dear and sympathetic being who seemed to be a part of one's own self. He had despaired of finding such, until
. .

The unfinished sentence had hung upon the air. Morag had been afraid to think too much about it.

In return she told him a good deal about her own life, and his heart was wrung with pity when she described her desolate, unloved childhood, the more so because it was related matter-of-factly, as though it was nothing out of the ordinary. He was interested in her account of Amy

Dudley, and privately considered she had been as much thrown away on her husband as Morag was on hers. The Queen's enigmatic character intrigued him. Greater, nobler and more courageous than other women, she yet must be, he suggested, the slave to caprice, for otherwise how was it that almost overnight, Morag, whom she had jealously treasured and secluded from the world, had been suddenly sent away from her? It was not in accordance with other facets of her character.

But to this change of heart there was no solution, though Morag fancied that Elizabeth might have become disappointed with her because she was devoid of any real ambition.

That led to talk about her modelling, and Morag had promised to show him the puppets she had locked away in a box and had brought with her to Linkfields. It was a promise she had not been required to fulfil, for although it had been accepted that they would meet and continue their friendship, even after Guy returned and she left Quince Hall, that had not come about. Soon after, Stephen had abruptly left for London, though she had understood he intended to stay until well into the summer.

Since she had self-control she had betrayed no distress or disappointment when Erica, riding over to see her, had told her with regret that Stephen had gone and she knew not when he would next visit Quince Hall. Erica, observing her calm, was satisfied that despite Stephen's admission, Morag had no understanding of his state of mind.

Certainly Morag did not suspect that the news of her pregnancy was responsible. No word came from Stephen, but that she scarcely expected. It might be misconstrued if he wrote even briefly to another man's wife. But a faith had sprung up in her heart, and she did not believe it had meant nothing when they had talked of friendship and he had told her he was for ever at her service. Other men might make pretty, meaningless speeches, but not Stephen. She was convinced that were she ever to be in sore trouble she could call upon him.

Inevitably, as the months passed, he slipped into the background of her mind, for her thoughts were now centred upon the babe who would be born to her late in the year. Guy was kinder to her now, and looked upon her with content as her shape thickened. He consulted an astrologer said to be infallible in his prophecies, who assured him that the expected infant would certainly be a male. Morag, relieved of her husband's rough, perfunctory love-making, could be effortlessly friendly with him when they were together, which was seldom, except at meals, and not even always then, for Guy frequently entertained his men friends, and on those occasions Morag's presence would not have been considered fitting.

When that happened, Morag was always happy to sup with Joan Brownstone, who, although she made no comment, was affronted by the behaviour of Rose Yarrow.

It was bad for her mistress to be disturbed in her mind now that she was with child, and Joan was glad that she *could* be blind to the relationship between her husband and Rose, though it was impossible for her waiting-woman to be unaware of it. The servants, who admired Rose for her successful effrontery, kept up only the flimsiest pretence of respect for Morag. If any of them pitied her it was with contemptuous pity as a poor thing who was of no importance except as the mother of the expected heir.

Joan thought it good policy to be on friendly terms with the underlings at Linkfields, and she took trouble to be kind and helpful, though at first they were all inclined to shun her. But she had poulticed one girl's poisoned finger with an infusion of herbs of her own concoction, and had taken the pain and swelling from a stye which had closed down one of the scullery-maid's eyes. After this there was more friendliness, and although Rose had little to say to Joan, the young maid whose throbbing finger she had eased and who had occasionally helped Morag with her toilet before Joan's arrival sometimes talked freely to her. This girl was inclined to show some sentiment for Morag, and taking her tone from those about her, one day remarked with a sigh, that she was unlikely to survive the birth.

Whether or not it was Rose Yarrow who had spread that opinion Joan could not determine, but it vexed her mightily, especially when the girl, Emmie, revealed that Rose had an ancient great-aunt known as a wise woman, who lived in a hovel on the outskirts of the village. To this unprepossessing beldame Rose took presents—liquor and food and money—and Granny Sellers in return had promised her a splendid future. The young Lady Erskine's star was already on the wane, but Rose's was in the ascendant.

Supposed witches were feared and hated, and every now and again a fearful retribution might be exacted for their fancied crimes, but Granny Sellers had a reputation for benevolence and none wished her ill.

"But did Mrs. Yarrow of herself tell you this?" asked Joan, giving Rose the honorary prefix generally accorded to domestics in a superior position.

Emmie was somewhat confused. "We-ell, no, but I overheard her and Mrs. Stiggs talking one day when they were in the still-room and the door on the crack. I went there for rose-water for my lady, she having emptied her bottle."

Mrs. Stiggs was the cook, and Joan accounted her a low woman, though she was careful to keep that opinion to herself.

"They are as sorry for my lady as the rest of us," said Emmie, who, simple girl that she was, no doubt believed it. "The master is of an uncertain humour and was often harsh with her, but now he is kind, and we are all glad of it, for her last months of life are like to be happier because of it. 'Tis Rose who is the mistress here, save for name, and although Granny Sellers did not say so outright, she must have meant that when her ladyship dies, Rose, who is my cousin, will be mistress in all ways. 'Tis well known that the master had much fondness for her, even before he wedded by the Queen's command, which was a sad thing for them all."

"How so?" Joan, though seething with anger and conscious of a lurking fear, spoke carelessly, not looking up from the pressing of one of Morag's kirtles, and Emmie, while she chattered, continued to polish a fine old oaken chest.

"None dare disobey Her Majesty," said Emmie, awed by the thought of the great Queen whom she had never seen, "and the master was poor, with this great house deserted, and would have fallen into ruin. He had no choice but to take her ladyship, and she none neither. 'Tis said she fell out of favour with the Queen, and that 'twas either banishment or to be sent to the Tower. The master pitied her, belike, or it could be it was the money she brought with her . . . that I know not, only that for my cousin Rose and him 'twas the severing of two true hearts."

Little enough severing, thought Joan indignantly, whether
not their hearts were true. She had never before listened
patiently to such a gabble of nonsense, but it was nonsense
with a germ of truth in it, and for that reason she did not
put an end to it. Emmie was innocent of all evil intent, but
Joan felt a deep distrust as well as a deep dislike of Rose
Barrow. It was evident that she was hoping for, even
counting on, Morag's death in child-bed.

Joan had scarcely spoken to Guy, who had grudgingly
given permission for her to remain at Linkfields; but she
had disliked him on sight. Morag had told her little or
nothing, but Joan had pieced her story together, and was
indignant at the neglect and unkindness she had suffered.
This, probably, had so numbed her that it had not crossed
her mind that Rose was the primary cause of it. That
would have been impossible to one more shrewd, but to
Joan it seemed that Morag was as dreamy as the child
whom Amy Dudley had loved.

Yet in other ways she had changed much, and in her own
fashion she was beautiful—so kind and loving, also, that
Joan, who had felt protective to her after Amy's death, was
now deeply devoted to her. She did not believe that Morag
was particularly delicate, nor that her life must needs be
sacrificed when her child was born. "Not with me to look
after her," mused Joan, who had more trust in herself than
any midwife.

She had picked up a variety of knowledge, was naturally
intelligent, and, being the eldest of a large family, had twice,
when no midwife was forthcoming, helped to bring young
others into the world. It was true that these births had
been straightforward, and her mother had been able to tell
her what to do, but Joan had been praised afterwards for
keeping her wits about her.

Now she thought of her mother with respect, as one who
was meticulous and enlightened and without fear. Mrs.
Brownstone had insisted that in childbirth, dirt was the great
destroyer. Before her lying-in the humble cottage room had
been scoured. There must, she had instructed Joan, be an
abundance of hot water and clean cloths. Joan had scrubbed
her own tending hands until they had felt raw and the cotton
dress she had worn had been speckless. Content with a clean-
ness which most would have thought excessive, her mother

had come through her two ordeals with calm and confidenc
and since Joan's father was a relatively well-to-do farmer bot
babes had been welcomed with joy by their parents.

Joan now reflected that her mother, who was of muc
the same build as Morag, had said that it was not alwa
the large, plump women who had an easy time. She ha
had a poor opinion of midwives, often sluttish creatur
insisting on an unlimited amount of ale for their own su
tenance. Joan determined that she would keep a hawl
like eye upon the midwife, who was one of Rose Yarrow
cronies, and fortunately there would also be a leech in atte
dance.

Meanwhile Joan was concerned that the months of waitir
should be pleasant for Morag, and she did her best
think of diversions for her. In this, Erica helped. Sl
visited Linkfields, never less than twice a week, taking the
both for airings in the family coach, and sometimes t
spend hours at Quince Hall. Morag was making most of th
baby clothes. Joan cut out the garments from patterns pr
vided by Erica, and sewed the seams. Morag embroider
sprays of flowers and clusters of fruit. Interspersed wi
hours of dreamy content there were hours of restlessnes
but Joan believed that moderate exercise was beneficia
and sometimes they would walk beyond the grounds and alor
the country roads. Morag would have liked to be on friend
terms with the families of the tenant farmers, but she w
given no encouragement. The women plainly avoided he
or if they could not they spoke to her in dour monosyllable
They were a strangely unfriendly community, thought Joa
not realising how unpopular Guy's father had been.

It was now, though grudgingly, allowed that there w
some improvement. Stiles, the new bailiff, was set again
evicting those who could not or would not pay rent for t
occupation of cottages which were little better than hove
These, when possible, were being repaired, and the thatch
was kept busy with roofs which should have been renew
months before, as was the glazier with broken windows. B
local memory was long, and Guy did nothing to ingratia
himself. False reports of Morag herself were spread abroa
She was a lazy, fine lady, who sulked because she was
longer at the Queen's court. She took no interest in h
household and had imported " a foreigner " to wait on he
The local housewives of the better class despised her becau

she had not dismissed Rose; those who were low, ignorant and coarse—and they, as in so many secluded English villages, were in the majority—also despised her as a " nothing," and admired Rose with her triumphant airs, her fine clothes and the lavish way in which she would distribute largesse to even her most remote relations. Of these there were dozens, and they all fawned upon her, fully believing that she would soon be mistress of Linkfields.

As for the county families, nothing that Sir Richard or Erica could urge, not even their acquaintance with Morag when they met her at Quince Hall, could induce them to countenance the régime at Linkfields, and in several cases there was anger because the men-folk accepted invitations to stag parties there, where much heavy drinking was the routine. Staid and usually pious ladies agreed that Morag was gentle, intelligent, modest, all that a young wife should be, and that it was pitiable she should have married Sir Guy Erskine, evidently having no knowledge of his loose character, but nevertheless unless she succeeded in reforming him, it was impossible to visit her or to extend hospitality to her. The poor girl had been forced into an outcast position, and it was hoped that when her child was born she might, with the status of motherhood, acquire sufficient authority to hold her own as mistress of her household.

In the event, Morag was to make some such effort long before it was expected of her.

One summer evening when Morag knew that Guy was giving a supper and card-party to his men friends, she, who had every intention of keeping to her own apartments, remembered that earlier in the day she had left a book she was reading on a seat in the garden. Joan would have fetched it for her, but she was in her room, writing a letter home, and Morag thought it a shame to disturb her. She went down the stairs rather heavily now, as was her wont, and saw through the open dining-room that the table was set festively with glass and china and lighted candles. That was more of an elaboration than was usual when Guy entertained his friends, but it would have had little significance for Morag, except that at the head of the table, in the massive, high-backed, tapestry-upholstered chair, which Morag knew had been the chair always used by Guy's mother, Rose Yarrow was now installed.

It was not only this impudence but the girl's proprietary air that struck Morag. She sat there proudly, one hand with a gleaming ring upon it, fingering the stem of a half-filled glass. She was wearing a gown decidedly unsuitable for one in her position. It was of an emerald-green silk, cut low, leaving her plump shoulders bare. There was a glittering jewel in her hair and a gold chain about her neck. Morag stared with amazement upon this grandeur. She walked into the room and confronted Rose.

"What happens here?" she asked.

The woman did not rise or show any sign of respect. A derisive smile lifted her lips. "Naught happens for the next twenty minutes by the time-piece, or perchance more if the men linger at the tavern, though that they will scarce do, since they can drink their fill here with no cost to themselves, mean-natured as most men are."

Incredulous, yet with no fear of her, Morag said with an authority she had never before shown: "Mrs. Yarrow, you much mistake me when you adopt such an insolent tone. But you are not yourself, and to-morrow will be cast down with shame, for having helped yourself to your master's wine."

Rose retorted scornfully: "My master! Aye, in a sense he is that, though not in such sense as yours."

To Morag this made no sense of any kind, but her temper was rising. She said: "You are tipsy! Get to your room and take off that dress and those gauds. It might clear your head to put it in the rain-barrel. To-morrow, when you are yourself, I will deal with you."

"*You* deal with me?" Rose rose leisurely to her feet. She had certainly taken wine and was not entirely sober, yet her mind was not so clouded that she was unconscious of what she said.

"Who else?" Morag asked calmly.

"If I take rebuke from any, which is not my habit, I take it from Guy, though he is not like to side against me."

"From . . . from . . ." Morag could not believe that she heard aright. Surely no drink-bemusement could wholly account for such insolence.

Rose was now beyond all caution. To see Morag scorning her, and addressing her as any mistress might be expected to address an impudent servant, was too much for her. She uttered a hearty oath and cried: "Aye, 'twas Guy

I said, and that's what he's been to me for years, and long before he set eyes on you. My lover. Guy . . . who'd be fit to slash his throat across did he think I'd leave him. You are here to breed, and 'tis to be hoped you're good for that, if for nothing else. Now get you back to your own quarters, and leave me to mine. I sit at the head of the table this evening, as oft before."

"You must be mazed in your wits," Morag uttered, but she knew it was not so. Rose was only slightly tipsy, for she stood steadily on her feet and spoke clearly, and what she said was the truth. Morag stared at her in horror and Rose laughed. There was a cruel pleasure in inflicting such humiliation after months of tendering a grudging respect.

To Morag, that loud, coarse laugh was the culminating insult. A tide of nausea surged over her, but she quelled it. For half a minute, which seemed ageless to her, she stood clutching the back of a chair; then abruptly she turned and left Rose in victorious possession. Morag's one desire was to set a far distance between them. She felt as though she was being stifled, yet she shivered. As she stood in the great hall breathing heavily, it was as though the walls closed in upon her, and the high ceiling lowered to press down upon her. With a gasping sigh she pulled open the heavy main door and was out in the open. The evening air fanned her cheeks. It was starting to rain, but she did not heed it; all her urge was to escape.

She started to run, making instinctively for the least-frequented part of the grounds—the little wood beyond the lake, where the conifers grew thickly and would afford her some shelter. Her breath came in gasps, and her heart was thundering. A dull pain had started to gnaw at her, but she scarcely noted it. Twice she stumbled over hassocks of grass and was brought to her knees, but she pulled herself up and ran blindly onwards, though the rain was now falling heavily. She reached the lake and could go no farther, though in the confusion of her mind she did not recognise that softly rippling sheet of water for what it was, and but that her strength gave she would have plunged into it unknowingly. Her knees buckled under her and she fell on the brink, her sense of identity lost, and desiring only oblivion.

It was some time before Joan missed her mistress. She had left her quietly resting, near to sleep, and it was not until the letters to her mother and her aunt, which were a monthly duty, had been written, that she returned to the sitting-room, to find it empty. At first, that was no cause for alarm. Although of late weeks Morag had rarely left her rooms unaccompanied, there was no compulsion on her to stay in them, and she might be in the library or the picture gallery, both favourite haunts and rarely if ever entered by Guy or any of those to whom he extended hospitality.

Therefore, Joan waited for Morag without anxiety, but when she glanced at the time-piece on the mantel and saw that it was near the supper hour, she decided to go in search of her, for soon the servant girl whose duty it was to wait on them would arrive with the tray sent up from the kitchen.

But the picture gallery and the library were both empty, and now Joan was concerned. From behind the closed doors of the dining-hall came the sound of loud voices, splutters of laughter and an incoherent snatch of song. Joan frowned in disgust. She knew well that Rose Yarrow would be presiding at this unseemly banquet, for with his wife conveniently kept in the background the master of Linkfields had given up all pretence of decent behaviour.

Joan grieved for Morag, was indignant for her, and wondered passingly what would befall her in the future. It might be that the coming of the child, if it proved to be a son, would see a change for the better but Joan doubted it. The tenants of Linkfields were a graceless lot, and their landlord little better; they were looked down upon by those on the Quince Hall estate, who regarded them as not much more than savages. How could Morag expect to win over either her husband or these ignorant peasants while Rose Yarrow was in power, giving such commands as pleased her and liberally favouring her indigent relations and friends?

One day Morag would have to know of it all, but not, Joan prayed, until she was well and strong again. Now Joan wondered where to search for her. In the past she had sometimes mounted the spiral stairs to the tower, for the sake of the fine view the narrow windows afforded, but this she had avoided since the heaviness of her pregnancy. Could she possibly have gone out into the grounds? Surely not, for although it was only just twilight, the rain was falling heavily. Having searched the tower room in vain, and looked with a growing desperation into every room that had an unlocked door, Joan intercepted a footman who came out from the dining-room with a tray of used glasses and dishes.

Through the open door she caught a glimpse of Rose Yarrow lolling in her chair, with her cheeks flushed and her gown in disarray. Guy, who had left his own seat, was feeding her from a bunch of cherries, several of which he had twined in her hair. A cluster slipped into the sagging front of her gown, and to the accompaniment of ribald laughter Guy plunged for it.

Disgusted, and angry beyond fear of offending, Joan tersely told the footman that she was in grave anxiety for her mistress, who was not to be found throughout the house. The master must be told, and a search made for her.

Called away from highly pleasing sport with his doxy, Guy was at first irate, but although he had taken much wine, from long dissipation he could carry his liquor better than most men, and at length Joan's anxiety communicated itself to him.

When Rose, petulant at his prolonged absence, joined him in the hall and heard that Morag was not to be found in the house, she made light of it, though in truth she had received a shock which more than half-sobered her. The fear came upon her that she had gone too far. Guy's tallow-faced wife was of value to him in her present state, and if he came to hear of what had occurred there might be retribution.

Now Rose berated herself for her incautious tongue and for the urge to humiliate Morag which swept over her. It was certain that the wretched creature when discovered would tell all.

But perhaps she wouldn't be discovered—alive. Perhaps in her despair she had done away with herself. Rose, belatedly aware that it would be prudent to show some anxiety, could only hope so. A self-sought death would be an easier way of ridding herself of her rival, than through a spell brought about by her great-aunt, or the midwife's blunder during her delivery.

With an urgency that surprised Joan and galvanised Guy into activity, she insisted that there must be a search of the grounds, the fields, the neighbouring countryside, in which all the servants and such of the guests as were fit to stand on their feet must take part.

TEN

Twilight was merging into the darkness of night before Morag was found. At first when she was seen lying on the brink of the lake she was thought to be dead, and it was still in that belief that her rain-soaked body was carried to the house. But when she was laid upon the settee in the great hall, it was discovered that although unconscious, she still breathed, and a manservant was sent on horseback to summon the leech. By the time he arrived Morag had been carried to her bedroom, where Joan, with the help of the tearful Emmie, took off her soaking clothes, dried her icy body with warmed towels, and tucked her into bed with a hot brick at her feet.

Morag struggled from oblivion, to a pain such as she had never imagined. At first in panic fear she believed she was dead and in hell; but then Joan's kind and worried face swam into her zone of vision and she clutched at her. Bright lights shone upon her, there was the confused babble of voices. She could remember little of what had occurred, and did not realise what was happening to her. The only reality was the convulsion of pain that racked her body. She prayed for relief, and as from a far distance heard Joan's voice, telling her she must be brave and patient and all would be well.

At this comforting, the leech shook his head disapprovingly. He did not believe in buoying up a patient with false hopes. Her ladyship, though her life hung in the balance, might possibly recover, but there could be no hope of saving the babe who was arriving three months before the rightful time.

" She does not even know that her pains have aught to do with the babe," said Joan. " Her poor wits are all awry."

The local midwife was attending the birth of twins to a matron at some distance, and the leech, finding Joan sensible and able to help, had said there was no need of her. The guests had all departed. Guy was pacing the great hall in a frenzy of disappointment. He cared little for Morag, but much that his son would be born too soon for a hope of survival.

Rose, to the surprise of all, had succumbed to a fit of hysteria, and was now sobbing weakly but continuously. Guy stopped in his restless striding to regard her with irritation.

"What ails you? 'Tis no grief to you that ill has befallen her."

"'Tis shock, and the pity I feel for you in your need of an heir."

Guy said with bewildered anger: "She was strong and thriving until foolery brought her to this pass. 'Tis beyond all comprehension why she should have roamed so far from the house, and then have laid herself down to die, with the rain pouring on her. Could she have had it in mind to drown herself in the lake? But why so? There's no reason in it. She was happy at the thought of the child, and there was kindness between us. Not even for you would I be harsh, when her well-being depended on a smooth passage."

"She could not have meant harm to herself. She must have been in a fever," Rose muttered.

Hysteria had been brought about by rage and fright. If Morag recovered, she would without doubt tell Guy the truth, and he would then cast blame on Rose for the premature birth. He might even break with her, his desire for an heir being so obsessive. She would be turned away from Linkfields and there would be no more adulation for her cleverness and her success. Those she had queened it over would deride her in her downfall, for they had no real love of her, only self-seeking. Luck, thought Rose, had turned against her.

Only one thing now could put matters right for her, and that was Morag's death. But Dr. Rice, the old fool, said there was a good chance she would live, though she must be in a parlous state. Leeches, however, did not always prove to be true prophets. Many and many a woman, when thought to be on the safe road after a birth, yet collapsed and died. Morag, through shock and such a drenching, let alone the unnatural birth, might well do the same. Once she was thought to be beyond danger, there would not be such constant attendance on her, and then . . .

"No," she lied, "but 'tis seldom I do see her these days. She keeps to her rooms with the Brownstone watchdog to see that none come near her, unless 'tis yourself, or any for whom she asks."

Morag, as an invalid recovering from pain and sickness, would, guessed Rose, be in no haste to see her reproachful and far from loving spouse. It would be a few days at least, perhaps a week, before he set eyes on her and she bleated out her story to him. Those few days were a respite to her rival.

"Well, she's young," said Guy, with an attempt at cheer. "We both are, and there's plenty of time before us in which to beget a family."

Rose bit her lips in a jealous spasm, not the less fierce because it would not be love which took him to his wife's bed. It was on her tongue to say cruelly that perchance Morag might be so injured that there would be no other children; but prudence silenced her. Guy would be wroth at such a saying, and the wrath might recoil upon herself.

She was conscious of a change in their relationship. Only a few months ago he had been so mad for her that she could act wantonly, tease him, play hot and cold as the mood took her, see him leave her in a tantrum, certain that he would abjectly return to her with a gift to win her favour. But of late she had with more difficulty beguiled him, and was aware that at thirty she had started to fade; there were lines about her eyes and mouth, and she was in danger of becoming too flashy even for the taste of a man who had no liking for a slender body.

Sympathy, and what she thought of as "coddling," were necessary, and now she set herself to comfort him by fond words and caresses. Her weaving thoughts were all of what could be done to silence Morag before it was possible for her to launch her accusations.

Morag grieved, but not with the intensity Joan had feared, when she was told that her child had been born too soon for a life separate from her own. Her weariness and weakness were such that nothing seemed of tremendous importance, and she was thankful for the peace, the silence, the comfort with which Joan surrounded her. For ten days she seemed to be making good progress, but on the third there was an alarming decline. A fever set in which Dr. Rice ascribed to the exposure she had suffered. Joan did not believe it. By this time she had no great opinion of the leech's capability or skill, and remembered the little faith her mother had had in them. Mrs. Brownstone and Joan's

Aunt Tansy had their own remedies for such illnesses as were well known and prevalent, such as the ague, feverish chills and the setbacks after childbirth. There were herb infusions which relieved a burning restlessness, and these Morag was coaxed to take. She was given light but nourishing food, and the room was kept at an even heat.

Rose Yarrow now made ingratiating overtures, not to Morag, but to Joan, who she was sure from her manner knew nothing of what had occurred. Joan, being no coward, would, Rose knew, have attacked her fiercely had Morag said a word to her. She concluded that Morag was either still too ill or too badly frightened to confide in anyone.

When Rose offered to night-watch, remarking that Joan's eyes were red-rimmed through nights of scanty, fitful sleep, Joan refused, but with civility. Emmie had already asked to be allowed to share the watching. Rose retorted that Emmie would certainly fall asleep once she was seated in a comfortable chair, with only the light from one candle since a brighter light might keep the patient awake. Joan, however, was certain she could trust Emmie.

Rose accepted that, did not prolong the argument, but on the evening of Emmie's first vigil she waited until Joan had thankfully gone to bed, and then softly knocked on the door of Morag's room. Emmie opened it, and was astonished to see that Rose, who rarely spoke to her unless it was to rebuke her for some duty left undone, was carrying a supper-tray. She smiled at Emmie with the utmost friendliness, saying: "You'll stay awake the easier if you have a full stomach. Here's fresh-baked manchets with cold mutton slices and a tankard of ale for you."

The gratified Emmie thanked her. She had a hearty appetite, and had soon eaten every scrap of the tasty supper, washing it down with the strong ale. Before long she was nodding drowsily, and when Rose cautiously peeped into the room she was sleeping sounder than Morag, who, though not awake, was tossing restlessly.

Rose, who had doctored the ale with a powder warranted to cure sleeplessness, was well satisfied. For a half minute she stood beside the bed, reflecting sourly that it was in this vast four-poster that Guy had made connubial love, and would do so again in another attempt to provide himself with an heir. This, if Rose had her way, should be thwarted.

Morag looked very small in the big bed, and although

103

said to be making good progress, seemed to Rose so frail and white and thin that a strong gust of wind might well blow out her spark of life. And that was what she should have, Rose decided grimly; not one gust, but hours of cold and spattering rain which would surely finish her. She walked across to the window and opened the casement wide.

It was a stormy night and the wind was moaning around the house. The branches of the trees danced an eerie dance, and the rain which had lashed against the panes was soon driving into the room and against the bed, though it was set a few feet away from the window. In the distance, thunder rumbled. Emmie's chair was sheltered by a screen, and drugged as she was, it was unlikely she would awake. As Rose quietly left the room, the candle was blown out by the wind. Rose went to her own room, knowing she would not be disturbed by Guy, who was at a neighbour's house and would not return until dawn. She fell into a sound sleep, hopeful that her plot would succeed.

The last person she had expected to baulk her was Guy, but his evening had proved to be tediously dull; the host, who was to be married on the morrow, was love-sick, with little heart for the traditional drunken orgy, all his being concentrated on the pretty girl who would soon be his wife. He had taken it upon himself to break up the party at a reasonable hour, paying no heed to the jeers and expostulations of his guests. Guy, cursing his host for a poor-spirited fellow, rode back to Linkfields as the storm reached its zenith and a white glare of lightning lit up the façade of the house.

Glancing upwards, he saw the casement window of Morag's room swinging back and forth. Either it had broken free from the hasp, or Rose had not securely fastened it when she opened it. Guy naturally knew nothing of this, but, not being fuddled, he realised that in such a storm the entire window, frame and all, might soon be torn out by the wind and would break on the stone paving beneath. He yelled for the groom who was expected to wait in the portal to take his horse at whatever hour he returned, and when the yawning, shivering fellow showed himself Guy dismounted, gave the horse into his charge, and was quickly within the house, in which, as might have been expected, all the inmates had retired and were presumably sleeping.

As another hurricane of wind hurled itself against the

walls and windows, Guy leapt up the stairs, and shouting out curses, burst into Morag's room. He caught the window as it strained on its last unbroken hinges, and, strong though he was, had some difficulty in dragging it back and bolting it. He had scarcely done so before he was joined by Joan with a cloak thrown over her night-gear, and it was she, not Guy, who took in the details of Morag's soaked bed, the quenched candle, and Emmie sleeping heavily in her chair.

"Fools that you are!" Guy stormed. "What are you about with windows open on such a night as this? Glass panes take a mort of money to replace."

Joan, though she had been so suddenly aroused from sleep, was wide awake, and her concern was not for possible damage to windows, but for Morag, who was not sleeping now, but staring as one in a nightmare at her husband, who had not approached her for weeks. Fortunately, as Joan observed, she had in her restless sleep thrown herself to the farther side of the bed, which was not wet from the rain. Holding Morag in her arms, Joan faced the irate Guy. "'Tis the danger to her that is most matter," she cried. "The window was fast closed when I left her to get the sleep which the leech said I must have after so much sick-watching. This fool girl was to watch in my stead."

"She sleeps sound," said Guy, with more mildness than was now usual to him. He was, in fact, sobered by the change in Morag, having not seen her since the night when she had been found unconscious by the side of the lake. Now after weeks of illness she was so thin, so fragile, that he could have fancied her transparent. Her eyes were enormous in her pinched face. It seemed scarcely possible that she was the girl he had wed with at least some semblance of desire. Now she resembled a wraith. "'Tis to be hoped your mistress takes no harm from this damp and chill."

Joan was wrapping a blanket about Morag. She had no attention to spare for Guy. He, had not Morag turned her face from him, would have said a kindly word to her, but her aversion was so evident that he was glad to retreat, leaving her to Joan's ministrations.

Having no suspicion that his intervention had ruined Rose's design to bring about a further serious illness which Morag could not have survived, he was perplexed when on the next day, Rose, being told of how he had come upon the scene, burst into tears. which were naturally supposed to be caused by a sympathetic concern.

"In faith you are much given to blubbering these days," Guy exclaimed.

Rose, beside herself with exasperation, hid her face in a kerchief. That he, of all people, should have saved Morag, was an additional aggravation, but she said between her loud sobs:

"We are both women. I have pity for her. She has no more fitness to care for herself than has a kitten. If I were Joan Brownstone I would give that slothful Emmie a sound whipping."

"Aye, she deserves it," Guy agreed, "even though it seems her mistress is none the worse to-day." He glanced at Rose discontentedly, for a weeping woman had never been to his fancy. "Come, dry your eyes, and I'll take you to the fair at Brenaby."

"Folk will talk to see us together," said Rose, who, although bold enough in her own village, where she was admired, could be abashed by the cold, contemptuous gaze of those living beyond it, who knew Guy and would have been his friends but for her.

"What matter? And 'tis not likely any of your betters will be at the fair, since they think such frolics beneath their dignity."

Rose shot him an angry glance. At one time he would not have dared to use such a phrase. She clenched her teeth in resolution. Once Morag was dead, and dead she soon should be, by another means since this last scheme had failed, she would coax or compel him into marrying her, and that would see a return of the old adoration, for it would be she, not Morag, who would give him his heir.

Joan was not angry with Emmie. She questioned her closely, but did not reproach her, nor tell her she was making untruthful excuses when she said tearfully that she had not opened the window, which had been fast closed while she ate her supper behind the screen. The storm had been getting up even then. So why, asked Emmie tearfully, should she have been such a girt fool as to open any window? Her cousin Rose, whom she referred to with respect as Mrs. Yarrow, had brought her a supper-tray, a most condescending kindness and welcome, as otherwise she'd have slipped down to the kitchen to get food, which would have meant leaving her mistress for a few minutes. As it was, she had not been out of the room at all.

"But you fell asleep," Joan said, not accusingly, but as a statement.

Emmie hung her head, muttering that she couldn't think how that had come about. She'd been wide awake, as lively as a cricket—she'd had a good sleep in the afternoon as Mrs. Brownstone had advised. She couldn't make it out about the window, for the bolt had been drawn fast. "I dunno what could have come over me," Emmie said, "an' I don't sleep heavy at any time, but I did then. Mayhap I walked in my sleep as I've heard tell folk do. . . ."

"But you never *have* so walked?" Joan asked.

Emmie shook her head. She had not, but it was the only explanation that occurred to her. Joan was thoughtful, and inwardly disturbed, though fortunately Morag seemed to be none the worse, which must surely be because the window had been open for only a short while and she had lain at the farther side of the bed where the rain had not touched her. Uneasy suspicions surged through Joan's mind. There was the supper-tray and Rose. It was most uncharacteristic of her to go out of her way to do any underling a kindness. But how could there have been real purpose in her action? How could she have been sure that the food and drink would cause Emmie to fall into a heavy sleep? Once she did sleep, it would have been simple for anyone to steal in and open the window upon the inclement night. Joan decided that as soon as might be, she would see Erica and ask permission to speak to her privately ; then she could tell her of the doubt and fear that nagged at her.

Emmie was abjectly penitent, but Morag, in her weak voice, told her not to fret. She was getting stronger every day, and would soon be about again.

She did her utmost to look forward to this, grieving though she was for her lost babe. Guy visited her one day, the first day that Dr. Rice said it was permissible for her to sit up in a big chair by the window, through which the sun now poured in.

Now Guy could see some semblance of the Morag who, when she was the Queen's ward, had briefly taken his fancy. There was a faint colour in her cheeks, and Joan had arranged her hair in soft loops and curls to frame

her face. She still looked as fragile as an egg-shell, but
there was no doubt that she was on the way to health.
Guy did his best to be kind. He would, he said, take her on
a trip to London when she was sufficiently recovered, and
the change would restore her. Perhaps the Queen would
extend an invitation to them both to visit at Richmond,
where the court was temporarily in residence. He had
written to Dudley telling him of their ill-fortune.

"We might—could we go to the play?" Morag asked,
her thoughts turning to Stephen. whose comedy must now
be at the stage of rehearsal. She would give much to see
it, and perchance she might even see him.

"Why not?" agreed Guy.

Morag found it an easy thing to read his mind. He
would be kind to her now, make pretence of solicitude,
because, desiring an heir, he needed her, and would make
love to her again in order to realise his hope. She shuddered,
for nothing now would induce her to consent to the marriage
relationship. At present she was too weak for the ugly scene
which must transpire when she told him she knew of his
relationship with Rose Yarrow and revealed that Rose's
taunts had sent her nearly demented so that she had rushed
from the house not knowing or caring where she went. She
would delay that scene for as long as she could, and then . . .
Surely there must be some way of putting an end to this
sorry farce of marriage. If she could see the Queen she
might pity her and help her. Morag believed that she would.
Separation, even divorce, was not unknown, though the latter
was rare and considered a sore calamity for any woman. But
no calamity could be so dreadful as a pretended reconciliation in order that Guy might beget through her.

He might be equally glad to be done with her, for from
the first she had been a disappointment, though how could
it be otherwise when he had loved the flamboyant Rose for
years? In any case, Morag reflected, if she could hold him
off, the visit to London would be desirable, for the Queen
would scarcely refuse to see her. She hadn't been sufficiently
grateful to Elizabeth, for how thankfully now she would
agree to study sculpture in Holland.

When Guy left her that day, it could have been the old
Guy of whom she had been mildly fond. He bowed
over her hand and kissed it. "Be of good heart, for already
you start to bloom again." he said, and was well satisfied
108

when he felt the small, thin hand tremble in his and saw the faint colour deepen in her cheeks. If he was to have a family by her, it behoved him to be more gentle and attentive in the future. Although he had as yet no intention of discarding Rose, he might possibly set her up in one of his smaller farms, and played with the notion of marrying her off to some old dotard who for the sake of a roof over his head and such extra comforts as Guy could bestow would turn a blind eye to the relationship between his landlord and his handsome young wife. Rose might not take kindly to the scheme, but Guy had little doubt she could be persuaded to fall in with it.

When he left Morag's room Rose was hovering in the hall, and the gaze she turned upon him was searching and secretly apprehensive. She had failed in her attempt on Morag's life, and since then had had no further opportunity to harm her. Now at last the meeting between husband and wife had come about, and although she expected an explosion of wrath from Guy, if nothing worse, she would meet it with defiance.

To see him come down the stairs with a self-satisfied smile was the last thing Rose had expected.

" How is she, then?" Rose asked.

" Looking a deal better than I thought to see her, and with the sense to listen to the leech and believe him when he told her it was a common thing for a young wife to miscarry with her first and afterwards to beget a healthy brood."

That was not precisely true. Dr. Rice had no doubt said as much, since he had thus endeavoured to reassure Guy, but when these consolations had been repeated to Morag, she had received them mutely.

" 'Tis but sense to cheer her and look to the future, instead of dwelling on the past," Guy went on. " A new gown, a trinket or two, a visit to Town, will soon see the end of repining. Mark what I say—before the year is out her ladyship will again be expecting, and it will then behove us all to take greater care of her. Not a step beyond the door, without one in attendance on her."

" 'Twas Brownstone's fault that she was unattended," said Rose, to whom it was now evident that Morag had revealed nothing of the scene which had sent her stumbling from the house in horror and disgust and misery, though why she had not taken her chance of casting the blame on Rose was a mystery.

"As to that, 'tis doubtful if her ladyship would be alive to-day, but for Brownstone's skill and care. The girl has done well. There are a dozen or more lazy, over-fed wenches here to act the watchdog when required. Brownstone, though devoted, is but human, and needs her hours of rest, as she also needs one under her on whom she can depend —not that feckless young cousin of yours. I have a mind to take advice from my Lady Adrian, who may know of one older to recommend, perchance trained in her own household."

"'Twas not my doing, but Joan Brownstone's own choice that fell on Emmie," said Rose defensively, "and 'tis not Brownstone who has berated the wench with falling into sleep when on duty. I threatened her with dismissal, but was then told that her ladyship had a liking for her and was unready to part with her."

Guy shrugged indifferently. "Well, leave it as 'tis for the time being," he said.

Rose put a hand on his sleeve as he would have brushed past her. "Dost blame me for what went amiss?" she asked, not with anger, but with humility which was the measure of her new self-distrust.

He stared at her in astonishment. "How should you be held to account for such misfortune? What ails you? I vow you have lost half your colour."

"Is that so strange when I have grieved and suffered for you?"

"Have you so indeed? 'Tis unlike you." In this new guise Guy was far from understanding Rose. He was flattered, yet was conscious of loss, for when she was scornful and headstrong, apparently caring nothing if she kept him as a lover, he had admired her and been stimulated by her. With meekness, half her charm for him evaporated.

Puzzled, and with no wish to linger, he pinched her plump cheek and told her to be about her work, as he could not that day spare the time for dalliance, a statement which, although teasingly uttered, stirred the embers of Rose's fiery independence.

"If you lack time, there are others who have more," she retorted, the old flash in her eyes.

Guy laughed. "Mayhap we will talk of that anon. If

he be unmarried he might yet make an honest woman of you, handsome jade that you are!"

He strode towards the stables, calling out for a groom to saddle his horse, and Rose, who gazed after him, knew a sinking of the heart. Even in jest he had never before uttered such ominous words.

ELEVEN

Although on the surface all was peaceful, a sense of tension rested over Linkfields. Morag was unwilling to bring about a crisis. When she saw the Queen, if Elizabeth would consent to see her, she would have a clearer conception of the future. Though the Queen might capriciously have tired of her—and that seemed to be the only explanation for the autocratic speed with which she had been thrust into marriage —she could have had no wish to punish one whom she had made her ward, one who had never consciously offended her. Elizabeth's sense of fairness was a salient characteristic, though there were occasions when for political reasons she was forced to act ruthlessly. But to one so unimportant as Morag she could afford to be kind, even though her fondness had waned. She would never, Morag was now convinced, have commanded this marriage had she known Guy's true character, or that he had an established mistress lording it over Linkfields who would hate any wife of his and make her life one long and constant humiliation.

Morag now looked back upon the years at Windsor with a sick longing. How thankful she would be if she were given some humble position in the Queen's household, for as mistress of Linkfields she could not believe there would ever be any particular happiness. Not long ago she had thought that to have a child would be sufficient for content, but though she grieved silently over her lost babe, she was resolved to have no more children by Guy, though the capacity to give him a family was her sole value to him.

As for Stephen, although she was conscious of the tender affection that had sprung up between them, it was dangerous to dwell on it lest the urge to throw herself upon his chivalrous compassion overcame her. If she gave way to that it might ruin his life, might even mean his death, since Guy, for pride's sake, would almost certainly challenge him, and in a duel Stephen, who so far as she knew had no skill with either rapier or pistol, would probably be killed.

He is safe so long as I am strong, thought Morag, and was convinced she could be strong, even to the extent of meeting him in London without betraying more than friendship. That, after all, was the only pact they had made, and what could be more innocent?

As health returned to her, ambition such as she had never known in the past slowly burgeoned. She did possess an unusual talent. All had said so, and if she could show the Queen some outstandingly clever example of her work, Elizabeth's interest might be kindled afresh, and as a patron of the arts she might think her too valuable to be wasted. Morag now realised that in the past her lack of any desire to use her gift as more than a pastime must have been irritating to the Queen.

With that in mind, she called upon Joan to bring her the great chest in which she had stored away all her models both finished and unfinished, together with the supply of wax from which she had fashioned them. She had not lost her skill, she knew, for although she had used only clay when making the animal figures for the farm which had so delighted Erica's children, she had been slightly surprised by her dexterity, having never before attempted to model animals.

The two girls unpacked the contents of the chest, and Joan, who had not before seen any of Morag's work, exclaimed in wonder. They cleared a table, and set out the little figures, which after the lapse of time now struck their creator as being eerily lifelike. There were those which she had copied from paintings and miniatures, and the few which with reluctance she had modelled from people who were actually alive. At the model which was a miniature facsimile of Guy she gazed with covert distaste. Although only a little over a foot in height, it had, or so she imagined, a curious vitality. She remembered how it had amused her to dress the little figure, sewing the tiny garments to the formless wax trunk, which because it *was* formless, seemed to her to deny it identity. But once the clothes, made of scraps of rich material supplied by Mrs. Ashley, were fashioned, they disguised the formlessness. The velvet doublet with slashed sleeves, the long, fine hose, the buckled shoes of felt, were

n almost exact replica of the garb worn by Guy, and the
attitude of the manikin, hand on hip, head proudly reared, was
is attitude. To Joan it was the outstanding model in the
collection.

" 'Tis a marvel, 'tis scarce to be believed, mistress, that
one taught you this craft," Joan said, " but the figure of
he master appears to be the only one you have taken from
a living person. This, now," and she lifted a puppet with a
kirtle sewn with dozens of tiny glittering beads and wearing
an enormous gauze ruff, " is I imagine of poor Lady Dudley."

Morag's expression was sad as she gazed at the model.
" Yes, but I was never satisfied with it, and showed it to
none. I kept it in a box by itself. 'Twas modelled partly
rom my memory of her and partly from the miniature
painting in the locket she gave me."

" 'Tis like enough to her," said Joan, still lost in wonder,
" but it must surely be easier to model from one who can
give sittings as though to a portrait painter."

" Easier . . . yes, but within me there is a dislike—a kind
of fear. I know not who told me or if I read of it, but
tis said to bring ill fortune to be modelled in wax."

" Methinks I also have heard that," said Joan, struck.
" It is old witch lore, and who can say if there be truth
in it? It is said that if a secret enemy makes a wax figure of
he one he hates, and then puts a curse on it and exposes
he wax to the sun or the heat of a fire, that person dwindles
and fails as the figure melts; and when 'tis no more than
a small pool of wax, he dies."

" I had not before heard it related so exactly." Morag
shivered slightly. " But it's . . . horrid. I have no belief in
such a fantasy, yet it makes me loth to use a living model.
When that has been pressed upon me, I have only modelled
he head and hands and feet with accuracy. The body is
. . a nothing. The Queen knew of this—she thought it
nonsensical and would have laughed me out of it. I
remember telling my husband, though he wasn't my husband then . . ."

" And did he so laugh?"

" He did indeed and mocked me for giving a second thought
o it. Oh, I expect it did sound childish and ignorant . . ."
She broke off, for there was a knock on the door. A
servant announced Lady Adrian. Erica, in riding-dress.
greeted Joan with a smile and warmly embraced Morag.

"My dear love, how much improved you are. It gladden my heart. Soon you will be sufficient strong for the sho coach drive to Quince Hall."

"Oh, I am sure of that, and I should enjoy it above a things. It could not possibly set me back."

Joan went to fetch refreshments from the still-room— sponge fingers and the home-brewed raspberry cordial whic both Erica and Morag favoured. Erica turned her attentio to the display of wax models and was lost in a wonder ment even greater than Joan's. The animal figures tha Morag had made for the children had impressed her, bu they were but childish toys; these perfectly-fashioned model were not.

"I know naught of such things," Erica said, "but I hav belief that you could if you set up in a business, make fortune for yourself, as do successful painters."

"But I would not know how to start."

"It is but a foolishness to discuss it, since your positio in life forbids such enterprise, but were it otherwise yo would, I suppose, require advice; perchance what is calle a middle-man to barter for you. How astonished Stephe would be to see such clever work. I had a letter from hir yesterday. He is in great concern for you. When I las wrote to him, I told him of your illness and that you . . ."

"That I had lost my babe? Do not fear to speak o it. It sometimes, although so recent, seems so much i the past, that it might have happened in another life. have shed so many tears there are none left, but I sometime feel it was good fortune for the babe to know naught o this sad world."

"But Morag, darling, it can be a happy world," Eric protested.

"Yes, for you, and I am glad of it, but this babe woul have grown up with his parents at strife with each othe It would not have been a good life for a child—force presently to realise that his mother was held of sma account, and that an evil slut was the real mistress of Linl fields."

So her eyes were open at last! Erica scarcely kne whether to be glad or sorry. It was a sorrowful thing see such bitterness twisting Morag's small face and th storm in her eyes.

Morag was thankful for the sympathy and understandin

f Erica's expression. It was as though she had been dumb
ince the evening when Rose had lashed her with insults,
ut now her lips were unsealed, and with a hard brevity she
old Erica of what had happened. "I cannot," she said,
" for much longer abide beneath the same roof as Rose
Yarrow, and need not, now my strength is returning. Guy
plans this visit to London, and if I can hold him as now,
at a distance, then I will accompany him, and by good
fortune may be able to lay my case before the Queen.
She could not have known—there were years when she
cherished me, though I did not deserve it."

"If you loved her, 'tis like she took pleasure in it," Erica
ventured. "Mayhap a Queen needs personal love more
than a subject—the universal worship with awe can scarce
be as warm and comforting."

"It was Amy I loved. I know not how I felt towards
the Queen. 'Twas near hatred at first, but that passed. She
was wondrous good to me. I could not but be grateful to her,
though not sufficiently so. I should have told her . . ."

"Told her what?" Erica asked. But to this question,
Morag only shook her head.

Joan Brownstone was loitering in the drive, and presently
when Erica came riding her horse towards the road leading
to Quince Hall, Joan moved forward to intercept her.
Erica pulled up. Could her ladyship spare her a few minutes,
Joan asked, and when Erica assented, she helped her to dismount. They walked slowly down the country lane, Erica
leading her horse.

Erica said: "You are worried, especially worried—but
why? Your mistress is well again, or nearly so."

"In herself, yes," Joan agreed, "but she is in danger.
That Rose Yarrow would have her dead. 'Tis my belief
that she has already made an attempt upon her life, though
I have no proof."

Erica listened in silence to Joan, as she had listened in
silence to Morag, hearing this new story of the storm, of
the open window when Joan had been forced by sheer weariness to leave Emmie in charge. " 'Twas she—Yarrow—who
stole in to open it," Joan said. "Who else would so have
done? And that girl—Emmie—was given something to
make her sleep heavily. Why else would Yarrow, who holds
herself above giving any service, who does but order the

other servants, have so demeaned herself as to bring a supper tray to the girl? I doubt not it was the spiced ale, in which a potion would have been tasteless. That she failed will not baulk her for long. My lady, I live in dread of what fresh scheme may be hatched, for 'tis impossible to be on guard every moment of the day."

"Should you not lay these suspicions before your master?" Erica asked.

"But would he hearken to me, caught as he is by that woman who is scarce to be matched for wickedness? Even if he did give attention, he would not believe."

"Joan, we cannot be sure of that. It might be the turning point for him if he once came to fear for his wife's safety. Failing Sir Guy, you might mayhap warn her."

"How could I thus scare her when she has been so ill and knows nothing?"

"Ah, but there you are wrong. She does know, but shock or sorrow has held her silent. Only just now she told me . . ."

Joan listened, her face reddening with indignant wrath. "Had I but known, I would have been fit to kill the woman!" she cried. "To think that 'twas through her the poor babe was lost!"

"Persuade your mistress to tell her lord of it," Erica advised. "She should have done so ere this, for the woman will doubtless deny it all, and the long delay in accusing her will give her denial some substance. Your mistress means to break all this to her lord when they are both away from Linkfields, in London. It will be easier, she supposes, when he and Yarrow are separated by distance."

"And so it may be. She will not be able to lie and excuse herself and cajole him, and I know my mistress hopes for an audience from Her Majesty, who, having loved her well, will surely protect her."

"But this visit cannot be for a sennight or so, and if Rose Yarrow has any fiendish plan in mind . . . Much can happen, Joan, within a few days."

"I know it, my lady, but my mistress, though so gentle, is not to be easily turned, once she has made up her mind, and it seems she has thought this out during days in which she was too weak to do aught else but think. But as she knows that wanton for what she is, I can warn her, and

116

with the twain of us on our guard there will be the less danger."

"Make some excuse and sleep at nights in your mistress's room," Erica advised. "Give it out that she is still subject to fits of delirium. Who can prove otherwise? Not even the leech, since after childbirth many a woman is disturbed in her mind for months."

Joan agreed to do that, and Erica, wishing she could have given more positive instructions, at length remounted her horse and rode away to Quince Hall. It occurred to her later that she must write to Stephen and apprise him of Morag's impending visit to London with her husband. He would be angered if the visit took place, and ended, and he with no knowledge of it.

Erica was now conscious of a divided mind where Stephen and Morag were concerned. She was frightened for Morag, so much in need of the protection her dissolute young husband denied her. If Joan's suspicions of Rose Yarrow were justified, if Morag's life was threatened, if she were to die suddenly and inexplicably . . .

At this thought it was as though Erica's heart turned over, and she discovered then that her fondness for Morag swept aside the moral concepts which had been drilled into her in her youth. The *ménage* at Linkfields was impossible, and it was equally impossible to believe that all marriages were sacred. This particular marriage had been by royal command, forced on a young and singularly innocent maid, no doubt with good intent. Under such circumstances could it not be annulled by the Queen's wish, when she discovered all that had transpired? It seemed to Erica that there was a hope of this; a hope that Stephen and Morag might finally find happiness together. In any case she—Stephen's sister—could not plot and contrive to set up a barrier between them. Stephen was no young, heedless boy, and he must do as seemed meet to him.

It did not occur to Erica to consult Sir Richard, who knew nothing of the secret attachment. His advice could be foretold. He would tell her to take no part in any such matrimonial tangle: nor would she, save to let Stephen know that the London visit was imminent.

A little over a week later, Morag received her first letter

117

from Stephen. It was but the second she had had since her marriage, the first being from the Queen, who after a silence of months had, hearing of her disappointed maternity, written to express a sympathy in which there was little of queenly remoteness but much of womanly understanding. This was a prized letter, which Morag had read with gratitude and would always treasure; but her emotion then was as nothing to that with which she now broke the seal of Stephen's missive. Yet he wrote briefly enough, addressing her as Honoured Lady, and telling her that he had but just read a letter sent by Erica through which he heard that Morag and her husband proposed to visit London in the near future and to stay there for some days. He thus begged leave to offer hospitality. There were unoccupied rooms in his house, which were conveniently situated, and it could comfortably accommodate Morag and her waiting-woman, and Sir Guy and his valet. There was requisite stabling for horses and coach. He hoped much that he might have the honour of acting as host to his sister's good neighbours and friends.

The letter was entirely formal, yet Morag sensed a warmth in it, and knew well enough that such an invitation would never have been tendered to Guy alone. Would he agree? After some pondering she handed the letter to Joan, asking her to give it into Guy's own hand when he returned with Stiles from an inspection of new cottages which were being built on the estate and were near completion.

Guy was in no good mood after the inspection. It was a chilly day with a drizzling of rain, and he had had to descend three or four times from his horse to the mud-rutted lanes where the cottages were in course of erection. Stiles had had considerable difficulty in persuading him to agree to the building of these, insisting that some of the crumbling old cottages were beyond repair, and finally convincing Guy that in the long run those newly built would pay for themselves, as they would be let only to dependable tenants paying a fair rent for them. Guy had grudged the outlay, and cursed the labourers, whom he deemed to be finicky beyond belief, demanding as they did something better than mud-floored, windowless hovels and refusing to pay rent for them; nevertheless, he had been obliged to give in.

Joan, with a curtsy, proffered him the letter as he strode

118

into the great hall. She delivered it, she told him, at her mistress's bidding. Guy dismissed her with a curt nod, and Rose was at his elbow as he read the letter. He considered it, and then gratified her curiosity by relating its contents.

Although he had spoken to her of this proposed London visit, Rose had given little heed to it, supposing that it was unlikely to come about, since it would be undertaken chiefly for Morag's sake. Now that it appeared to be a certainty she was jealously angered, though on the same instant it occurred to her that Guy might be coaxed to take her instead of Joan Brownstone. She put this to him, employing her most persuasive manner, insisting that she could care for Morag as well as Joan could, and that some such treat was due to her. She had never set foot beyond her native village, longed avidly for the gaiety of London and its many sights, and was also mindful that her local prestige would be enhanced by such a visit and all she would be able to tell of it.

It was gall to her when Guy without hesitation refused to consider such an exchange. Her ladyship, he said, would certainly dispute it, and in this instance he could not gainsay her, since her health was still precarious and Joan had the nursing skill which Rose lacked. Moreover, Rose had always objected to waiting on Morag. In time past nothing would induce her to do so.

Rose bit her lip to suppress angry retorts. Not long ago Guy, if obliged to refuse her, would have been apologetic and contrite; but now he dismissed her plea as though it was of little account. With his thoughts reverting to the expense of building the new cottages, he remarked that Stephen's invitation would be a saving on inn accommodation, which was in many cases far from comfortable. The offer of hospitality was one which he appreciated. The Adrians had ever been good neighbours, and no doubt Lady Adrian's brother had been prompted to his offer by his sister's suggestion.

"Think you so? It seems more like that it is unbeknown to her, and that he has seized upon it as the chance to see more of your lady wife," said Rose spitefully.

Guy stared at her incredulously. "You must be astray in your wits. For all your spleen you know well enough that her ladyship is innocent of all guile."

"So she may be, but a London gallant could have his desire fixed on her, seeing more beauty in her than you see. When he was staying at Quince Hall last spring, so was she, and you away with my Lord Dudley. 'Twas common talk that he dangled after her."

"That dull dog with his books and his learning and his playwriting, lamed as he then was, and older than her by several years! Who told you this?"

"The second footman—Pell; he left soon after, to better himself as butler to Lord Hepworth in Bath. But he was here when Joan Brownstone arrived, and took her along to Quince Hall. He seed her ladyship coming out of the woods with this Master Clinton, and her arms full of flowers and he looking at her, said Pell, as if he couldn't look enough."

"So, 'tis naught but servant's tattle, as I might have known. As like as not my Lady Adrian was with them." But although Guy brushed the insinuation aside, he was inwardly disturbed, having wit enough to realise that the invitation would scarce have been proffered to him alone since he had been hard put to it to show Stephen even a bored civility. But it was impossible for him to believe that Morag had shown favour to any. She was devoid of all carnality: matrimonial love-play, let alone its culmination, was a penance to her, as it was, so Guy had heard, to all virtuous women, to whom children served as compensation. For their husbands such licensed love-making was of little sport, and for himself no more than the necessity to beget a family. Only dull fellows were faithful to their immaculate wives, those of greater virility looked elsewhere for their pleasure, and of that he had had his fill with Rose, to whom he had been surprisingly constant. Although she no longer had the freshness of first youth, he might search far and wide before he found another to suit him as well.

On that appreciative reflection he took her arm and led her through the nearest open door, which chanced to be that of the deserted library.

"'Twill be but a short visit," he promised as he fondled her, "and by the time I'm on my homeward way, I shall be hungry for you, my lass. Who knows but that I might bring you a length of fine silk from Spitalfields. I trow I'd get the warmer welcome for it."

Rose was appeased because his mood had changed. For

120

once his ardour meant more to her than promised presents. Fool she had been to fear that he was tiring, but having faced the possibility of it, she gave herself to him with an abandon that was the measure of her relief.

TWELVE

Although Guy had scarcely listened to Rose's defaming words, they were not dismissed from his mind. Later, he brooded on them. It struck him that to a milk-and-water fellow such as he deemed Stephen Clinton to be, Morag might have her attractions. Why not, since even he, though only rarely and fleetingly, had been conscious of them? Certainly she was not ill-looking.

As a lute-player who had pleased the Queen with his melodious tenor voice, he had been obliged to memorise many a sentimental verse set to music, as well as the old roistering favourites. These verses all dwelt on love and the charms of the beloved, which were seldom of the robust variety. The sirens who were a poet's inspiration nearly always had alabaster skins, slender bodies, languishing airs and lustrous, swimming eyes. They cradled snow-white doves to no less snowy bosoms, had little feet that scarce pressed the daisies when they walked on the dewy grass, and to kiss their fragile hands was, apparently, the summit of the poet's desire.

Guy had sung of all this, generally with little thought, but sometimes with an amused contempt. Poets were not his boon companions, but it might be that there *were* such fools, who asked no more of the damsels they admired and courted. Stephen was a playwright, not a poet, but to Guy's mind there was little difference. Writing of any kind was a feeble business ; books, though as a boy he had been forced to pay them some attention, were the ultimate boredom.

Morag, when he now considered her, appeared to possess some of these far from stimulating charms. Her skin was certainly white and her shape slender. It was long since he had seen her smile or show a spark of gaiety, but her eyes were large and heavily lashed, though their expression was wistfully sad.

The sadness could be accounted for by the loss of her

121

babe, which had been a sore disappointment to him, more especially as it had been of the desired sex. It was, he supposed, grievous to her because she had longed as a child longs for a doll, for an infant she could dress and undress, caress and cuddle. That being so, and her health now mended, it would be to her happiness to find herself again with child. Guy assured himself with a sense of conscious virtue that although it was no great exhilaration to exercise his marital rights, it was as much his duty to Morag as to himself. The leech had assured him that there was no reason for denial, and although Morag gave him no encouragement, that no doubt was due to the confounded shyness which made her—to him—so unenticing.

Although Rose had satisfied him, he was, late that night, urged to break down the barrier which he had had no wish to demolish once he knew that Morag had conceived. A slight, pin-stabbing chagrin when he considered Stephen Clinton goaded him. If the fellow had a fancy for her, the sooner she was once more child-bearing, the better.

Morag, roused from a deep and dreamless sleep, uttered a cry as Guy's hand fell upon her shoulder, and he was momentarily taken aback when Joan Brownstone, also asleep on a pallet near her mistress's bed, awoke and raised herself upon her elbow. It had not entered his head that the waiting-woman slept in the same room.

"Get you gone," he said harshly, setting down the candle he carried. "Your mistress has no longer need of you during the night hours."

Joan murmured a stammering remonstrance, and might have put up an active resistance had Guy been in a drunken state, but he was not, and for once she was in perplexity as to how to act. It was not within her power, nor was it her right, to come between husband and wife, and Morag, for all she knew, might welcome a reconciliation. Her mistress settled the matter by saying quietly: "Go, Joan please . . . I am not afraid." Then, wordlessly, Joan gathered up her blankets and dragged the pallet into the adjoining room. Guy shut the door after her and turned the key in the lock. He came back to the big four-poster to find that in the brief while of his turning his back to her, Morag had slid from the bed and thrown a shawl about her shoulders. Now, standing, she faced him.

"Why should you be afraid?" Guy asked, forcing himself to gentleness. "Am I not your lawful spouse? We have been too long separated, sweeting."

"By your wish, as well as mine," said Morag.

"Nay, 'twas because of your sick state, but you are no longer sick, and 'tis time you forgot your grief and took hope. With good fortune, we shall have other children."

"No." She shook her head vehemently. "You will beget none by me. Ours was a marriage unwelcome to both; but the Queen, had she known . . . she would not have commanded it, had she known . . ."

"Known what?" Guy demanded.

If he had thundered the words, Morag felt confusedly that she might have respected a man's anger and humiliation at denial, but instead he shrilled at her in the tones of a sulky boy.

"That you had a mistress; a coarse besom on whom you set much store; that you put her over me to taunt me, and flounce herself to the scandal of the neighbours, who, rather than seem to countenance it, shunned me and would not set foot over the threshold."

"Who told you such? But 'twas Lady Adrian without a doubt—a haughty shrew, thinking none good enough for her company."

"She and Sir Richard were good to you," Morag said quietly, "when you most needed goodness. But from Erica I heard not a single word. None betrayed you, save Rose Yarrow herself. 'Twas she who told me."

"You lie!"

"I have never lied to you. She had drunk too much, and her spleen overcame her. She—it was she who near wrecked my reason, and so filled me with horror that I, not knowing what I did, only with the desperate need to set a distance between us, ran out into the grounds in the storm, and remembered little else before I heard my babe was dead."

Taken aback, Guy was for the moment speechless. Then —"You lie," he again accused. "If it's truth, why did you keep silent for so long?"

"I meant first to tell the Queen."

"The *Queen*?"

"Why not, since she it was who brought us together?

123

Perchance hearing all, she will in justice devise some mean by which we may both be free."

"You would not dare venture to reveal this to Her Majesty Nor would she hear you."

"I think she would hear me. She has much fairness. think she would not have me suffer for all my life, becaus I had no choice but to obey her."

"You are a fool," Guy fumed. "At the most, did sh give you audience and pay attention to your plaints, sh would but advise you to make the best of what you have and she might send for me to rebuke, and set us both off t a fresh start."

"How can there be a fresh start when we have no lov for each other, and there is this woman the sight of whom i as poison to me?"

"Her Majesty knows well that it is commonplace for man to keep a mistress; but since it is such distress to you I am willing to remove her from your presence and set he up at a distance. As for love . . . how many marriages, thin you, are based upon it? 'Tis rather on joint interests tha they prosper. Set but your mind on the management of you household and the rearing of a family, and you should b as content as any woman."

"No," Morag said.

Guy seized her in his arms. "You forget, madam, tha you owe me obedience as your husband, and that I am i power over you. Unless you yield to me there will be n visit to London, nor the chance to bleat your grievances t the Queen, though that methinks may be of less import t you than to dally with this playwriting churl, who doe but invite us to his house so that he may have the bette chance to cuckold me."

Morag strained away from him in disgust. She said "Your mind is foul and you are hateful to me."

"Hateful I may be, but you must accept me. If nee be I can keep you prisoner—and will. Who's to preven me if I shut you up in the tower room and send Brown stone about her business? I would be your only visitor, an how long, think you, would you hold out against me? Thi is no idle threat, for such could be done and more, if yo drive me to it."

At last Morag was terrified, and her eyes revealed it. H was cruel, heartless beyond measure. Guy, seeing her fea

124

was spurred on to further threats which should subdue her. "You shall bear me as many brats as I decree," he boasted, "though you'll not have the rearing of them, or the chance to make them as puny and whining as yourself. I'll get a woman who is a woman to mother my sons, when they're taken from you at birth."

"Are you then a monster?" Morag tried in vain to sound courageous and scornful.

How could one be courageous seeing a man suddenly turn to madness? Thwarted, Guy would be capable of any villainy. A wave of fainting sickness spread over her. She sagged limply in his hold, and but for it would have fallen. The livid colour of her face alarmed Guy. With a curse he threw her from him, and she fell upon the great bed, white and senseless. Guy stared down at her in a fury. It was as though he had held a fluttering bird in his hands, and pressing too hard upon it had stilled for ever the fluttering beat of its heart. He unlocked the door and called loudly for Joan Brownstone, and when she answered the summons, made her attend to her mistress, to tell her on her recovery that with the dawn he would be on his way to London, there to crave audience of the Queen.

To Joan this statement signified nothing, though she guessed it was of importance to Morag. She set about reviving her, while Guy who in expectation of a reconciliation had had little to drink that night, now applied himself to the bottle, whereby to forget his wrecked self-esteem. He was the more baulked because he was as enraged with Rose as with Morag. It was she, the boasting trollop, who had robbed him of his son, and had so turned Morag to bitterness that he might never relent and bear him another son. With all his flagrant faults, Guy was no rapist, and although a chilly, submissive wife was endurable, one clenched in hatred against him was not. That he had only himself to blame for Rose's presence at Linkfields, was a fact brushed aside. A pest on all women! They were treacherous jades, whether of low or high degree. Between these two he was helpless, and the message he had told Joan Brownstone to deliver was no more than an idle threat, though warranted to frighten Morag. His pride would never allow him to reveal to the Queen that his wife spurned him, but it would be balm to his injured spirit to seek out Stephen Clinton, insult him, and then challenge him to a duel for the seduction of his wife.

125

The fellow could not deny him that satisfaction, and Guy had no doubt but that he could either run him through with his sword or blow out his brains. As like as not the bookish lout had never handled a rapier, or a pistol, whereas Guy was expert with both.

This reflection and plan of campaign did something to soothe him. It would break Morag's spirit to know that she was responsible for Clinton's death, and might well turn the Adrians against her, thus depriving her of her only friends. At length, fuddled with wine, Guy sought his bed, and fully dressed as he was, threw himself upon it and fell into an uneasy sleep.

Morag came out of her swoon to find Joan bending over her, and with a wet cloth pressed against her forehead. There was no merciful haziness to cloud her senses, but an immediate, vivid recollection. She raised herself to gaze round the room and to recognise thankfully that Joan and she were alone. Then came tears of mingled relief and wretchedness and she clung to Joan.

Hitherto she had said little or nothing about her husband, feeling that she owed him that much loyalty, if nothing else, but now she was too lonely, too frightened, not to confide in Joan. All was sobbed out against her shoulder whilst Joan listened in speechless indignation.

"He will send you away from me, so he says. He will lock me up in the tower room, there to stay until I submit to him. But I never, never will. I would die rather. Oh, Joan, that is what will happen, for I had put all my hopes on seeing the Queen, and now I shall not be permitted to set foot in London, so the chance of an audience is denied me."

"Sir Guy," said Joan, "will soon be on his way to London. He bade me tell you that he would crave audience of Her Majesty."

"So that he may set her against me; so that she will do naught to help me, as might have been, even if the marriage could be set aside only by Act of Parliament."

"If your lord has a mind to complain of you to the Queen, surely in the fairness of her heart she will wish to hear you speak also?"

"How can I tell? I have never understood her rea

disposition towards me; but the memory of her kindness gave me hope."

Joan could offer scant comfort. Women by law and religion were subservient to their husbands, and she wished for Morag's sake that she had less aversion to hers. Had Joan been of a craftier disposition she might have urged her to cajole Guy, to pretend an affection she did not feel, to burnish her beauty, and so enchant him that Rose would lose her hold on him; but, proud of heart herself, she could offer no such advice. A hatred that rivalled Morag's was by now kindled in Joan. She had heard too much of a man's absolute rights to doubt that Guy, if he chose to, could carry out all his threats. She would be sent away, and there would be none to protect Morag from humiliation and despair.

The long night passed slowly. In the early morning, looking from the window, Morag saw Guy come forth from the main door, and a servant sent running to the stables. Presently Guy's favourite roan was led to the front of the house, likewise a horse for Kern, the valet, who usually accompanied him when he travelled. The latter brought forth baggage which indicated that Guy might be away for some days. Whatever his mission, that was welcome knowledge.

The two men mounted their horses, and instantly Guy was away at a gallop, his man having some difficulty in keeping up with him. But that was not unusual. He was a reckless rider, and although his valet had been chosen for his horsemanship as much as for his deftness in personal service, he grumbled openly over the treatment of the horses, who were urged on at speeds that soon had the poor beasts in a lather.

When the sound of the thudding hoofs had died away in the distance, both girls relaxed. Guy might be gone for a short or a long time, but even a few days was a respite. After such long and sleepless hours, Joan urged Morag to rest, and once stretched out on the bed she was asleep within a few minutes.

Joan, tidying the rooms, paused before a shelf in the powder closet where Morag's finished wax models had been set out. Once again the puppet figure of Guy struck her as singularly exact. She stood looking at it with a strange

expression. Witchcraft was sometimes justified, thought Joan
or at least it would seem so to a woman driven beyond all
bearing. She was no witch, and so far as she knew had never
met with one, but she could set a curse upon the waxen
puppet, and who knew but that it might work upon the
one who was the human version of it.

Words that she had scarcely realised she knew trembled
on Joan's lips, and were muttered just above her breath.
Were they to take effect, there would be no hope for Guy.
There was also the required melting of the figure, but that
would take too long. Joan had heard that the process
should be continued for a matter of days. First an arm and
then a leg, later the entire wax body exposed to the heat
of a flame. By such a process the withering of the real
Guy would also take too long. A great pest he would be
to everyone, while dying of a wasting disease, mused Joan
mercilessly. There was a better way, and she gazed around
the closet for what she needed.

The small chest in which Morag kept her jewels was
open. She was careless over such things, and it was Joan
who would remember to lock the chest and put the key in a
secret place; but such carelessness was welcome now, for
there among the little heap of gems, and the pearls which
had been the Queen's gift, was a long, sharp-pointed pin
—a pin ornamented with a fire opal set in pearls. Joan
had no idea that it had been Guy's gift to Morag before
there had been any talk of marriage between them—given
to her on an impulse of liking and gallantry; but if she had
known, she would have thought her action all the more fitting.
Taking up the pin, she tested the point of it, found it sharp
and for a moment debated with herself. Should she plunge
it into the stomach——? But men had recovered from such
wounds. Besides, sharp though it was, the thick velvet of
the tunic might be difficult to pierce. Belatedly she remembered that Morag had said the bodies of her puppets were
but formless lumps of wax and bore no resemblance to
humanity.

By this time the fantasy had caught hold of Joan, and
with half her mind she was believing in it. It was the head,
the face, of the puppet, that had been minutely fashioned.
And nobody could have mistaken it for anything but Guy's
face and head. Joan thrust the long pin through the centre
of the puppet's brow, with such deliberate savagery that

he point of it protruded through the diminutive wig that
covered the skull.

With satisfaction she stood back to gaze upon her handiwork. The opal head of the pin splashed colour on the waxen
forehead, and could have been some curious decoration.

Sanity slowly returned, and with it she sighed heavily.
Fool that she was, to have believed even for a minute in
such rubbish; but it had been her need for vengeance on
Morag's behalf—a passionate protest at her helplessness.
Ridiculous it might be, but she had savoured a moment of
power and triumph, though now she could laugh scornfully
at herself. Her hand went out to remove the pin. It would
leave but a small hole, and that she could cover by bringing
down the fringe of the wig. She was about to do so, when
Morag called to her from the bedroom, and, impatient with
herself and the fantasy of murder which for a few minutes
had seemed so real, so satisfying, Joan pushed the puppet
to the back of the row, where it was half-hidden, and then
obeyed her mistress's summons.

The day passed slowly. Morag slept fitfully for a few hours
and Joan watched beside her. When she woke, she prepared a meal for her and they took it together.

Much to Rose Yarrow's disgust, Joan had lately taken
it upon herself to cook Morag's meals, disregarding the
annoyance of the cook, who objected to the waiting-woman's
presence in the kitchen, and because she insisted on watching
while dishes were separately set out for her mistress. Joan
explained smoothly that her ladyship's digestion was still
weak, that her meat must be done to a turn and that were
were certain garnishings she could not stomach. The leech,
said Joan, had told her this was most important. That was
why it was better for her to take portions of fish or fowl
and steam or poach them separately, and since her mistress
had a liking for sweet things, to be sure the puddings were
not too rich for her.

"The eyes of a hawk that one has," grumbled Mrs.
Stiggs, " to watch her fiddle-faddling she could be afeared I
had it in mind to poison the pair of them."

Joan had no such fear of the cook, but a very genuine
fear that that might be Rose's design, and Rose suspected it,
seething with rage but wholesomely respecting Joan's acute-
ness. She had had it in mind, when Mrs. Stiggs's attention

was diverted, to sprinkle the special dishes sent up to Morag with a powder ground from certain berries which even the village children knew better than to pluck and chew but now she had abandoned the plan. It would be too hazardous, and might not have succeeded even if Joan had not been on the alert, since success depended upon how much Morag took of the dish, and her appetite was poor.

Who would have supposed that it would be such a hard task to put an end to the moping, skinny moppet, who looked to have no strength in her? But only that morning Emmie had unwittingly provided Rose with a different scheme. There was a swing in the orchard, and her ladyship, said Emmie, was, now that she had recovered her health, as pleased with it as a child might be. It was a marvel that she, being so delicate, was not turned sick and dizzy when she took a pleasure in swinging so high, almost up to the top branches of the trees. When Emmie had spied her at it yesterday she had had a heaving in her stomach but her ladyship had laughed, and when she had set foot on the grass again there had been light in her eyes and colour in her cheeks. "So pretty and not grieving for the babe any longer," Emmie said with sympathetic pleasure.

Now Rose pondered. Ropes of a swing could fray, and who could be called to account if they broke asunder? None had thought to examine the swing for its safety.

Rose was disturbed because Guy had departed so unexpectedly and so early, without a word to her, but now she was glad he was absent. If he was not there to demand her company, it gave her the more time. Suppose . . . suppose when he returned it was to find . . .?

The day-dream of Morag flashing through the air to lie motionless with a twisted neck on the rough grass was a sweet dream, but there was no certainty that some other might not take a fancy to use the swing after the trap was set. Try as she would, Rose could not think of how that could be avoided. To openly forbid this harmless sport might, if misadventure befell Morag, call an unwelcome attention to herself. There would always be such hazards, Rose realised, in plotting for a death that must appear to be an accident.

From a window, later in the day, she watched Joan and Morag strolling together in the garden, and presently they disappeared in the direction of the orchard. What ill fortune that she had not already severed the ropes, so that the swing was supported by nothing but a frayed shred, for now it was likely the swing would be put to use. But to do this work on the ropes, Rose would need the cover of darkness.

It was seldom that she had the opportunity to put her foot inside the rooms that were allotted to the mistress of Linkfields and her waiting-woman, for Emmie cleaned them, and Joan superintended her work, having made it clear that Rose's inspection as housekeeper was unnecessary. But now that they were at some distance from the house, she could gratify an idle curiosity, and even if either or both returned and found her there, what could be said? It was her duty to see that curtains were taken down and fresh ones hung at regular intervals.

She looked round the big bedroom and glanced cursorily into the small one leading off from it, which since Morag's illness had been Joan's. Both were orderly. The door of the powder closet stood ajar, otherwise she might have overlooked it, but now with curious eyes she gazed upon the delicate, fluted, silver-stoppered bottles that contained lotions and scented toilet water, and the small locked chest where Morag kept her jewels. Finally her gaze came to rest on the shelf where the wax models had been set out.

These much astonished her. She had never seen anything like them, and had no idea that Morag had fashioned them. She took up one after another to examine them. They were more than dolls, and who had ever heard of a grown woman, unless she was half-witted, playing with a doll?

Picking on one puppet to observe it more closely, Rose dislodged another that had been behind it. It fell on its face, and turning it round she uttered a sharp exclamation. A pin had pierced her finger, drawing blood. She sucked at it, and then her brown eyes bulged, for she was gazing at her lover's miniature effigy, and so exact that it was past belief. She did not immediately grasp the significance of the fire opal, pearl-surrounded, which glowed in the centre of the wax forehead. But then probing fingers again came in contact with the sharp point of the pin and she gasped. It had been run through the manikin's head, and if there had been a brain within it, that brain would have been pierced.

Who could have done this, other than the one she chose

to consider her enemy and rival? And didn't it show—didn't it plainly show . . .?

Suddenly, as she stood there, Rose heard a commotion without. The window was open, and not caring now if she was seen to be in Morag's room, Rose leant from it. There had been the sound of horse's hoofs ringing on the courtyard flags, a hoarse voice calling, the clatter of feet as grooms and servants came running.

Rose saw Kern, Guy's valet, swaying in the saddle on his sweat-lathered horse. The creature, brought to a standstill after hard riding, was trembling. One of the grooms caught at the bridle, steadying Kern with his other hand, as the valet half-fell to the ground. Then they were all clustering round him, hiding him from Rose's sight; but there was no muffling of the man's voice, which though broken and gasping came clearly to her ears.

"My lord . . . they are bringing him home . . . a wagon—it'll be here anon. He put the roan at a high hedge and it threw him . . . on his head. He was away before me, as always, but when I got to him, I knew. There wasn't a chance, falling so . . . the force of it . . ."

Waiting to hear no more, Rose tore from the room and ran pell-mell down the stairs. The magnitude of the disaster that had come upon her was instantly realised. Fury overspread any shadow of grief. She had lost all . . . all, and it was through his tallow-faced wife, who had used a witch's spell to bring about an untimely death.

Rose was still clutching the manikin in her hand. Now before she joined the throng in the courtyard she pushed it deep into the pocket of her skirt, and the hot determination for revenge rose up in her. If Guy was dead and she deposed, Morag should pay for it.

THIRTEEN

Morag could not believe that Guy was dead.

To her, it was at first no more than a particularly vivid nightmare, though she listened with seeming calm to the wretchedly miserable Kern when he described exactly what had happened. Guy had been riding, even more recklessly than usual, and in order to shorten the journey had taken

132

more than one by-pass across the fields, spurring his horse over hedges and gates, and jeering at Kern, who, good horseman though he was, was unable to perform such feats and had laboured after, keeping to the road. He had not, however, been far behind when Guy, with no regard for the tiring roan, had set it at the hedge which it had failed to clear. Falling, the poor brute had broken both its fetlocks, and Guy, pitched upon his head, had died instantly.

Kern, coming level with them, had seen at once that nothing could be done. With perhaps as much grief for the fine horse as for his headstrong, imperious master, he told how with Guy's pistol he had shot the writhing animal before riding to the nearest farm for help.

Later, a wagon from this farm brought Guy's body back to Linkfields. There it was laid on a trestle table set up in the great hall, and covered with a velvet curtain taken down from one of the tall windows.

Morag looked upon her dead husband with a dazed compassion, and no sense as yet that through his death she had acquired her longed-for freedom. The servants, headed by Rose Yarrow, filed past their master's improvised bier, but after that there was no sight of Rose.

Morag, with Joan, retired to her own rooms. There was sorrow of a kind. Morag, being tender of heart, grieved for Guy's wasted life, and remembered him as he was when first known to her. There was as well the sense of shock and complete unreality. Joan was the first to stir herself, recalling that Morag had taken no food since the early morning, when they had seen Guy ride off. She would now set about preparing a meal for her. After a while she returned with a laden tray, but with an expression so unusually disturbed that Morag questioned her.

"The servants have gone," Joan said. "One and all, from Yarrow to the scullery maids, they have left. Below, there is naught but disorder; unwashed dishes, fires half-out, and before they went, they raided the cellar and must have taken much liquor. We are alone in the house, mistress. 'Tis as though they fled in panic fear."

"But why? Not surely because their master lies here dead?" Morag rose up in consternation. "It cannot be that. More must be afoot than we know of—though now I recall when the sweating sickness struck down my husband's parents, those of the servants who were able deserted Linkfields; but that was fear of the infection. Is it because they hate me so much?"

It did indeed seem to both girls as though some poisonous vapour had spread throughout the house, and Joan, though she scarcely knew why, was afraid. However, she coaxed Morag to eat, and over the meal they debated what could now be done.

"It may be that the grooms and coachman are still in the stables," said Joan, "and there is Mr. Stiles, who would surely not desert."

"You forget—Stiles is ill of the jaundice, and not yet fit to leave his bed. But we cannot stay here alone, Joan. 'Twould be best if you went over to Quince Hall before dark falls, and tell them there of our distress and this desertion. I doubt not that Lady Adrian will come to me with such servants as can be spared."

"Come you with me," Joan entreated. "Even if there is no groom to saddle a horse, 'tis not too far a walk with my arm to lean upon."

Morag shook her head. She could not, she said, leave her dead husband alone, fleeing from him as though she feared him, who now lay beyond harming her in the great hall. If she so fled she would despise herself for a cowardly callousness. Joan, if she hastened, would not be gone for more than an hour.

Joan realised that she was determined, and that to argue with her only wasted time. She was beset by an inexplicable dread, and throwing on her cloak she swiftly departed.

Down the long drive she sped, and along the country road, but she had covered less than a quarter of the distance when there was a scuffling in a nearby thicket, and from it there sprang out a couple of men who roughly seized her. "'Tis the witch's servant," one cried, "who belike goes to summon aid for the witch herself."

Joan fought fiercely for freedom, crying out that Morag was no witch, but a gentle lady in sore distress at her lord's death. This statement provoked a roar of loud laughter. Even in the dim light, Joan recognised her assailants as two of the servants at Linkfields, employed to fetch in kindling for the fires, to clean boots and knives and do all the most menial tasks. They were ignorant and uncouth and brutally strong. One struck her a blow on the head, the other stuffed a filthy rag into her mouth to stifle her cries. Finally

oan lost consciousness and her body as limp now as a rag
oll, was tossed aside into the ditch.

ir Richard and Erica had travelled that day, Sir Richard
ding and Erica by coach, to attend a wedding some twenty
iles distant. They had left early in the morning and might
ave delayed return until late in the evening, but that there
ad been, that week, two separate parties travelling north who
ad been set upon by footpads. Having committed robbery
nd assault, they had then escaped. Until these scoundrels
ere captured there was a general disinclination to be abroad
fter dusk had fallen, and though Sir Richard, with a stout
scort all armed with pistols, would have braved danger for
imself, confident of getting the better in any affray, he was
indful of Erica's fear, which she could not hide from him.
herefore they left the scene of the merry-making when it was
ill at its height and arrived at Quince Hall to Erica's
reat relief without molestation.

When the coach was heard to rumble up the avenue, the
ain doors were thrown open, and Erica, tired by the long
ay and stiff after the drive in the none too comfortable
oach, luxurious though it was considered, was helped to
light. Barely had she set foot on the ground when a shadowy
gure which had been huddled against a wall flung itself
owards her and caught imploringly at her skirts.

Erica uttered a startled cry, and Sir Richard threw a
rotecting arm around her, as one of the footmen hauled
scarcely more than childish figure to its feet. He was
bout to fling it roughly aside when Erica stayed him.

"My lady . . . my lady, I beg you hear me," cried a
irl's voice, broken by sobs. "'Tis Emmie Bowles from
inkfields, and I have waited long to speak to you, after I was
urned away."

"Who turned you away?" asked Erica, and then said
o her husband, as the light from within the house fell on
he trembling girl: "It is as she says, Richard. I have
een her at Linkfields. She is employed there."

"I dared not leave a message, and they would not let me
tay," Emmie said. "I was afeard to return. If they knew
ey would be fit to kill me."

"Who would? Stop crying, child. None will harm you.
What was your message? What brought you here? Fetch
er within, Davis, and I will question her."

Emmie was in a woebegone state, her face streaked with grime and tears, and her teeth chattering. Erica regarded her with compassion, and Sir Richard said: "A glass of hot mulled wine for the poor wench. Seat yourself, girl, and take your time."

Emmie spluttered as she gulped the wine and gazed at them with terrified pleading. "But there has been much time lost already," she cried. "I know not what may have happened to my lady by now, and she alone there with Mrs Brownstone and the master dead! Nay, 'tis true, my lord, my lady. He was brought home tossed from his horse and killed, and all swear that 'twas my lady's doing through the spell she put upon him, but I—I love her who has ever been kind to me, and that I trow is a lie, for all the manikin that is the master's image, with a spear thrust through his head."

Sir Richard and his wife gazed at each other in concern, scarcely knowing whether to believe this ramble, wondering if madness had come upon the shuddering girl; but bit by bit the story was dragged from her and pieced together, and both judged it impossible that there should not be some truth in it.

They heard of Guy riding out in the early morning, bent for London, and how some time later his valet had returned with the dire news of the fatal accident that had befallen him. Emmie was positive he was dead, for he had been laid out on a table in the great hall, and the servants had all filed past to pay their last respects. But then Rose Yarrow had collected them, one and all in the kitchen; the grooms and stable hands and the gardeners as well, and those who could not crowd into the kitchen had stood beyond the open door and listened to her. She had shown them the waxen image of the master, and although but about a foot high, it had been his very self, dressed in such rich clothes as he usually wore. Rose had held it aloft that all might see. It was a witch's handiwork, she had said, fashioned so that the master's death might come upon him, for there was this jewelled pin run through the centre of the forehead, and was it not the injury to his head that had killed the master?

"Now," Rose had cried, "you are all like to starve, for she will turn you out, if so be she does no worse, forbearing to put her curse upon us all, so that we perish as cruelly as he has perished. But I have lost more than any of you, for this man was my lover, and was fain to put her away and marry me, who would have succoured you all for the love I bear you."

Exhausted by this long recital, Emmie burst into tears. Sir Richard was aghast, and Erica almost as white as the distraught girl.

"She is not mad," said Erica. "She speaks but the truth, and we, had we not been at the Nooth wedding, would have heard of the accident ere now. I have seen this puppet which so resembles Sir Guy. It was modelled by Morag long ago, before marriage was mooted. We must go to her forthwith, Richard. The poor, poor child to be there alone . . ."

Sir Richard continued to question Emmie. All the servants had scattered, she told him, and she had perforce gone with them. In the village, groups had gathered and vengeance been sworn upon Morag, who was a witch and should meet with a witch's death.

"They mean," said Emmie, "to tarry until 'tis dark, and then to drag her forth and drown her in the lake, unless she proves innocence by staying afloat and unharmed though her clothes be weighted down . . . but my lady cannot swim. I could not bear for this to be, and so I stole away, and none noticed my going. . . ."

Sir Richard put his hand on the girl's shoulder. He praised her. She had done well, and by God's mercy her mistress would be rescued. Dusk had but just fallen.

Then all was active, for commands rang out, and every male servant employed at Quince Hall was summoned. They were given brief orders, and those who could not ride were told to follow on foot. At the head of this singular cavalcade, Sir Richard rode forth, while Erica, left behind, gave orders that fires should be lighted and beds prepared for Lady Erskine and her waiting-woman. Emmie was given into the charge of a kindly housekeeper as unlike as possible to Rose Yarrow.

For Erica the next hour was one of painful anxiety, for although Sir Richard had done his best to reassure her, she was terrified that Morag might already be drowned by the barbarians who had banded together to destroy her. The events of the day were so unexpected and so tragic that her mind refused to assimilate them, but seized with eagerness upon any small task to occupy her and make suspense bearable.

Morag, in her shocked, stunned condition, was scarcely aware of the passing of time. She realised only as the day darkened that Joan had been absent for much longer than an hour, though she had said she would return with all speed.

While she was alone, Morag had wandered through the great empty house which echoed to the sound of her footsteps. She had never before encountered such a brooding silence. It was as though an immense black shadow hovered over Linkfields and was darker in the great hall than elsewhere. But she was not conscious of fear, only of desolation, and she longed for the comforting presence of Erica, who would understand even better than Joan that though she had not loved Guy, and although he had treated her ill, her heart was filled with grief.

All could have been so different, even without love, had he been different; they could have respected each other, there could have been friendship between them, and the mutual wish to make a success of their marriage could have brought harmony.

But the failure had not been solely Guy's fault, she thought humbly. She had been so ignorant, so unwilling, and so stupidly blind to the fact that Rose Yarrow's influence was evil. A wife of stronger character would have deposed her long ago, insisting that in the house where she reigned as mistress there should be no such insulting domination. Had she deliberately blinded herself, Morag wondered, caring little for Guy's neglect, but rather welcoming it because his attentions were obnoxious to her?

Candles were set around Guy's bier, and these she lighted. She knelt beside it, her heart full of sorrow for him. She should have refused to marry him. Not even by the Queen's command could she have been literally dragged to the altar, and no punishment devised by Elizabeth could have been so bad as that which she had suffered. She might have been banished from court, but could scarcely have been sent to the Tower. Deprived of the Queen's protection, she could yet have earned her living in some humble capacity.

She gazed at her husband's still and peaceful face. It was as if he slept. He looked even younger than he had looked in life, and he had had a passionate love of life. Greater

138

than mine, thought Morag, knowing that she would have cared little had she died when her stillborn child had been brought into the world.

She tried to pray as she knelt there, but prayer seemed meaningless, and God, though she did not doubt that He existed, seemed too far away to have concern for her.

Then through the maze of her unhappy thoughts, sounds from the outer world broke upon her. There was the trampling of feet, the babble of many voices, and at last a violent hammering on the stout oak door.

"Come out, witch," yelled raucous voices. "Come out, ere we break down the door and fetch you."

Not understanding, but terrified, Morag sprang up from her knees. The main door would hold against a battalion of hostile peasants, but there were the windows, which though latticed could be broken, and for all she knew the side doors might be unbarred. A swift glance from a ground-floor window showed her that at least a hundred had gathered without. There were torches which lit up faces distorted with mob passion, but she recognised them as those of Guy's tenants. Some of them bore iron spades and long staves with which they belaboured the door. She ran to those doors which led into the garden, but found them securely barred. Joan, before she left on her errand to Quince Hall, must have thought of her mistress's safety, and Morag blessed her for it. She fled up the stairs to the window on the first landing, which was above the main door, and, suffering a change of heart, she was suddenly fired by an indignant courage and threw it open. Silence fell upon the mob as they saw her standing there. She had snatched up one of the tall bier candles, which cast its flickering light upon her.

"Take shame to yourselves and begone," Morag cried in a clear, unfaltering voice. "Here your master lies dead with none to mourn him save myself, whom you, mad drunk with his wine, would molest. Have none of you respect or pity?"

"None for a witch who put her spell upon him and brought about his death."

It was a woman's voice, and Morag recognised it. Rose Yarrow, dishevelled, reeling drunk, her dress torn from her shoulders, pushed her way to the forefront. In one hand held aloft she waved the puppet figure which had served to inflame the mob. It was now scarcely recognisable, for many hands had torn at it and battered it, and Rose, recognising the value of the opal pin, had been sufficiently avaricious, once it had served her purpose, to tear it out and conceal it about her person. She had distributed wine from the raided cellar to all those ready to support her, crying out to them that if they were men not poltroons they would destroy the witch who had brought death to their lord and would be the destruction of them all.

"I had naught to do with this death, and now that my lord has gone, it is to me you owe your duty," Morag proclaimed.

This was greeted with a gust of jeering laughter. She shrank back as a heavy stone hit her on the shoulder. A volley of these followed, accompanied by shouts of encouragement:

"Stone the witch—stone her! Come out and face us, witch, if so be you are innocent. Stand the trial by water, or be burnt to a cinder."

Flames leapt up, and though it was only a flowering bush that had been set alight, Morag did not doubt that it was the prelude to a blaze which might fire the entire house. That part of it which was timbered would, she guessed, being old and dry, and with a strong wind blowing, burn readily.

Whether she lived or died, all engaged in this murderous affray would pay dearly for it the next day. The ringleaders would certainly be tried and condemned, and she shuddered to think of the bodies that would swing on gibbets, and of those who would be transported or would rot for years in prison. Her instinct was not only to save herself but to save the fools who had been led to this outrage by Rose Yarrow. But what could she do to save any of them?

A clear, cool thought came to her. Once more, braving the stones which might fell her, she stood within the frame of the window; and as though awed by her brave front, a silence fell in which her ringing voice could be heard by all.

"Good people, listen to me, I pray you. You have been led to this by her who was your lord's doxy, and who in losing him has naught else to lose; but you have much to lose, as those sober amongst you must know full well. I would not that you die and hang in chains for what you in your madness do to me and to your dead lord's property.

Go to your homes and keep the peace while still you may, and I as your lord's wife will bear no witness against you. But if naught but my death will satisfy, then that shall be brought about by my own accord and none of you shall suffer for it. . . ."

Rose Yarrow's scream broke the spell of silence: "She does but prate and think to bargain with her witch's cunning. Heed her not, fools that you be. 'Tis but justice that she dies. . . ."

"If that be so," Morag retorted, clarion-clear, "then because of the many who will suffer—wives and children who are innocent of all wrong—I will throw myself from this window to crash upon the pavestones where you stand, and none will be held to account. . . ."

Upturned faces stared at her, no stones were hurled; there was an awed whispering. "She lies, she lies!" shrieked Rose Yarrow. "She would fool you!"

Morag climbed upon the window-ledge. The wind swirled her skirts about her and blew out her hair. Fear had left her. She might be facing death, but at least it was death of her own choice, and of less horror than to be burnt alive, or to be helpless in rough hands which would hustle her to the lake and cast her into it to drown. The muttering below was rising to a growl, but the desire for her death was no longer unanimous, and when Rose continued to scream threats and abuse, those who stood near her turned upon her with sudden violence. One caught her by the throat, and her yell of protest died away in gurgling gasps. It was while Morag's fate thus wavered, that there came the timely intervention—flashing torches seen amongst the trees, approaching the house, as many riders galloped up the avenue. Then all was confusion. Horses driven ruthlessly amongst the crowd, scattered it as a scythe scatters blades of grass. Sir Richard's voice was heard raised in command. When, brandishing pikes, men thrust their way towards the house, some of Morag's would-be murderers fell wounded, some turned to fly. The man who had caught Rose Yarrow's throat in a throttling grasp cast her from him. She fell, and those who but a few minutes since had followed her lead, now trampled on her.

Morag, who had swayed on the window-ledge, knew that she was safe. For an instant she gazed upon the scattered stones on the floor-boards, only one of which had hit her. She was conscious then of a bruised ache in her shoulder, but that was of small account. Stumbling down the stairs she drew the bolts of the big door, and Sir Richard, crossing the threshold, caught her in his arms.

It was at that moment that Morag remembered Joan and said anxiously: " She went to fetch you, but 'twas long since. Did harm befall her?"

Sir Richard told her that Joan had been set upon by two ruffians, but by the time he and his men started out for Linkfields, she had recovered consciousness and had been seen crawling towards Quince Hall, though she was gagged and her arms were bound behind her. One of Sir Richard's tenants who was on horseback had left the cavalcade to ride back to Quince Hall bearing Joan to safety.

Within a few minutes there was not a rioter to be seen, for those who were whole had carried away with them those whom the pikemen had struck and wounded. Only one lay face downwards near to the bush that had been set alight and was still burning. Sir Richard's land-agent, who had brought out his pistol to fire a shot above the heads of the rioters (a shot which had terrified them more than anything else, though none had been hurt), turned about the fallen figure with his booted foot. The light of a torch revealed Rose Yarrow's contorted face. She had been strangled, though perhaps through accident rather than design. The puppet figure was still clenched in her hand, but it had been so trodden upon that it was featureless. The bailiff examined it uncomprehendingly, and then tossed it into the heart of the burning bush.

FOURTEEN

Morag was borne to Quince Hall, despite her protests. Sir Richard said he would leave a dozen of his men to stand on guard through the night. Thus due respect would be paid to Guy as the dead lord of Linkfields. Erica, he insisted, would not rest in peace until she had Morag safe beneath her roof. Thankfully she capitulated, and when Sir Richard praised her courage she was shamefaced because she now could not check her trembling, and was terrified because she must make the short journey riding pillion on his great horse. When she expressed her fear for his men, Sir Richard assured her that he did not anticipate further trouble from the rioters, who once broken up, were only concerned for their own skins; but even should the improbable happen and they banded themselves together again, his men, being all armed, would be a match for them.

Within a short while Morag was clasped in Erica's arms. In answer to her anxious questioning Erica told her that Joan had been tended and put to bed. Apart from shock and bruises she had not been hurt, though she was in great agitation on Morag's account. It was Emmie who had really been the one to save her life, and the girl had shown heroism, for she could have expected little mercy had she been discovered when on her way to Quince Hall to summon aid for her mistress. Now both girls were together, bedding in the same room, but they would not be likely to rest until they had seen her. Morag went to them, and Erica, watching her as she embraced first Joan and then Emmie and thanked them with tears of gratitude, wondered how it had been possible for anyone to hate her, or a husband to ill-use her. Morag promised that whatever happened they would all three stay together now. Emmie had earned her undying gratitude.

It was not until late that night that Sir Richard and his wife were able to retire. The news of the uprising had travelled to the nearest town, probably by word of mouth from some of the outlying tenant farmers, and a justice of the peace had called out the local militia-men to preserve order. They had arrived at Linkfields to find all disturbance over, but since Sir Richard's men were in possession they had taken the precaution to call at Quince Hall to ascertain the cause of the trouble. Some time elapsed before, regaled with ale and food, they left the household in peace.

Meanwhile Thomas Stiles had had himself conveyed to Quince Hall in the Linkfield coach, and though still with a skin as yellow as ripe corn, would not be content until he knew that Morag was safe. He had struggled from his bed, despite the protests of his frightened wife, prepared to tackle the mob single-handed and had arrived on the scene just as Morag had made her speech which he declared he would not be likely to forget for many a long day. " She did in truth," he told the Adrians, " offer to make a sacrifice of her life, which would throw no blame on them; and

143

methinks the churls believed her, for with my own eyes I saw their lust to kill die down in shame, and then one turned upon that strumpet Yarrow, and seizing her by the throat must have near if not wholly squeezed the life out of her, before she was thrown to the ground and trampled upon, when your men, my lord, scattered the mob. I trow there will be many up before the justice to-morrow."

"Nay, there will be few enough," Sir Richard prophesied, "and of those, all will be as innocent as the day, swearing that they took not part. As for my Lady Erskine she vows that in the flickering light she could recognise no individual face. You, a sick man, Thomas, with your wits fever-addled, can be scarce expected to do better."

The two men exchanged reluctant smiles. "If that is how my lady would wish . . ." Stiles said.

"I dare swear it is, and who should wonder, since to save the great grief of the hangings was what impelled her to valour. 'Twould be but a cruelty to add to her distress over Sir Guy's death, and I, for my part, am fain to shield a brave lady from further ordeal."

Only when Thomas Stiles agreed to keep silent was he permitted to leave, and by that time he was in his sickness so weary, that his desire to bring the miscreants to justice had waned to the point of indifference.

Sir Richard and Erica discussed it all in the privacy of their bedchamber.

"Think you truly, there will be few arrests?" she asked.

"Aye, few enough when they are weeded out, and as Morag will swear it is impossible for her to identify those who threatened her, there will at the most be but light sentences—fines and mayhap short sessions in the stocks. That will be as well, since she who provoked so much malice and strife is now of no harm to anyone."

"'Tis strange indeed that Morag who is of such a mild spirit acted thus," marvelled Erica. "I cannot but feel pity for her husband cut down in the flower of his youth, yet 'twill take but little time for me to rejoice at her freedom."

It was only when both were in bed and Sir Richard was on the verge of sleep that Erica, who had been turning restlessly, said: "There was that which I forgot to tell you. Joan Brownstone, when brought here in exhaustion and ill used, could scarce speak at first, but when somewhat recovered she told me that in an impulse of rage she implanted a pin in the forehead of the puppet which Morag had modelled in her husband's likeness. Also she put a curse on it. . . ."

"And does she in truth think that that had aught to do with Eriskine's death?" asked Sir Richard, now grudgingly awake.

"I think it weighs somewhat upon her conscience. I think in her place it might weigh on mine."

"I have a better knowledge of your good sense. Tell the girl, if her mind is so disturbed, to pray for the unfortunate man and to strive to forget her hatred of him. Above all, let her not speak of it to Morag, who has sufficient as it is to haunt her."

"I greatly hoped you would say that," Erica murmured, as the blessed tide of drowsiness stole over her.

All responsibility was now lifted from Morag's shoulders. For her own sake it was given out that she was more ill than she actually was, and thus she was not called upon to attend either inquest or funeral. For the latter, Sir Richard made all seemly arrangements, and a subdued tenantry followed in procession when their lord was laid to rest in the family mausoleum. As Sir Richard had prophesied, few punishments were meted out, and only to those witless enough to admit they had been amongst the mob who had threatened the mistress of Linkfields with death. As these few were manifestly not of the stuff of ringleaders, there was no desire to make martyrs of them. As for Rose Yarrow, public opinion was that the district was well rid of her, and her death was said to be accidental. Those who had fawned upon her in her lifetime were quick to forget her. Many were now out of work and a charge upon the parish, though such might be rectified when the new owner of Linkfields took possession.

He was a distant kinsman of Guy's, a farmer living in one of the northern shires. He was unknown to any in the district, but Linkfields being entailed, and Guy having died without a son, the estate was now his by right. Morag reflected that it must have come as a surprise good fortune to Francis Erskine, whom she had once heard Guy casually mention. He was a middle-aged man with a wife and a growing family, and must have thought it a remote contingency that he would ever inherit Linkfields, since his kinsman was young, only recently married, and in the course of nature likely to produce a family. Morag was unfeignedly thankful, now, that that had not happened. She hoped that she need never set foot again in Linkfields. She would try to blot out the memory of it, and all she had suffered there.

Although she would not be rich, neither would she be penniless, for the dowry left her by Amy Dudley reverted to her now that Guy was dead. Her plans for the future were vague, but Sir Richard and Erica both said pressingly that they hoped she would stay with them indefinitely. There was room and to spare for her and Joan, and Emmie could be usefully employed in the Adrian household. Emmie had never known such kindness as was now showered on her. She would be given light work, Erica promised, such as would make her the more proficient to assist Joan as a personal waiting-woman either to Morag, or if she left her, to any lady of quality. Sir Richard tentatively mentioned that a small manor house on his estate would shortly be available, if Morag cared to rent it. The present tenant, an elderly widower, had given notice of his intention to spend the evening of his days with his married daughter who lived in Devon. Morag gratefully asked for a little time in which to consider the offer ; but Erica, though she said nothing to her husband, had her own reasons for doubting if Morag would settle permanently in the district. She had already written a graphic description to Stephen of late events.

At Morag's request, Erica with Joan and a couple of her own servants went over to Linkfields to collect all Morag's personal belongings and to arrange for the temporary storage of such furniture as the Queen had given her as part of her wedding gift. Although Morag doubted if she would ever again wish to make use of the furniture, it would be an insult to the Queen to part with any of it. The new owner of Linkfields had written cordially to Morag, wishing to tender any possible help and saying that it would be some weeks at least before he could take possession of his estate and being only a poor man, he doubted that he would need more than a fraction of the present staff. However, there was little he did not know about farming, and his sons were likewise inclined, he therefore hoped to prosper. The small farm he at present owned was to be sold.

The Adrians doubted if such a family would be a social acquisition to the neighbourhood, but they would probably be preferable to either the dissolute late owner or his father. As for the servants of these, there were none, save the coachman and grooms and Stiles, and two of the gardeners who had humbly begged to be reinstated. These, by arrangement with the new owner, would be retained until after he took formal possession.

Morag heard all the details without much interest; but what did greatly interest her was the news that the Queen would almost immediately be paying a visit to Hatfield, making a detour on her way to visit a midland ducal estate where a great indoor pageant was to be staged for her and the scale of entertainment would be unparalleled. One of the Queen's secretaries had written to Erica to advise her that the Queen had signified her gracious intention to visit Quince Hall while she tarried at Hatfield. It was emphasised that the visit would be quite informal, and that no entertainment would be required or indeed desired, as the Queen's object was to rest for a short while before proceeding on her journey. Her visit to Quince Hall would be a private one of a few hours only, when, unless Lady Erskine was sorely ill, she would expect to see her. The Queen had heard with regret of Sir Guy's untimely death, and there had been various stories of marvellous happenings since then, which might have no substance but into which Her Majesty wished to inquire.

Although emphasis was laid on informality, such a letter was sufficient to throw Erica into a flutter. The Queen could not visit the home of her unhappy girlhood without civic greetings and the entire population turning out to welcome her. Real privacy was something which not even she could hope to command.

Now a tremendous scouring of Quince Hall was in progress, and Erica, warned that she would incur Elizabeth's displeasure if she even spoke of the proposed visit, much less invited her nearest friends to be present, was obliged to make the preparations she deemed necessary under a cloak of secrecy. She could confide in none but Morag, who was in an agitation half of pain and half of pleasure at the prospect of once again seeing the Queen.

"But I know she will expect naught out of the ordinary," Morag said, calling upon her memory of the Queen's

147

occasional love of dispensing with all ceremony. "There were times when she would throw aside her majesty and be as simple and domestic as any ordinary woman. To me, though mayhap it is a presumption to say so, she could as she listed behave as an elder sister. You must have known her with an equal intimacy when she was but the Lady Elizabeth."

"I did. Richard and I both did, but much has happened to change her since then, when she was pleased to be given only a limited freedom, to be allowed to ride over on her palfrey and to play tennis or try her skill at bowls. All such and more she could have at Hatfield, but it was a change for her to be here, I dare say, for she had always the fear of spies even amongst her closest friends, and must have been afeared to speak one word that could be misrepresented."

"She must be still that same Elizabeth beneath the panoply," Morag suggested. "It was the one untortuous facet of her character, though that is stranger and more wonderful than can be rightly assessed."

"She must have buried her true self deep," said Erica, and then added with a sigh: "I wish I did but know at what hour of the day she proposes this visit, for at any time, did I know, I could present a banquet which though less elaborate, would stimulate the appetite as well as any of the fantastical viands such as we hear tell are served up at the royal palaces."

"Oh, I can imagine . . . the tales spread . . . swans and peacocks' breasts braised or roasted. 'Tis all a nonsense. There were many long courses, but the viands were for the most part such as we ordinarily have, and the Queen was ever a sparing eater. I am certain, Erica, that you have no cause to worry."

But Erica was now all perturbed hostess, and there was much extra baking and checking of the contents of the still-room shelves in the few days before the Queen made her unheralded arrival at Hatfield. But as news invariably travelled swiftly by word of mouth, it was soon known that Her Majesty, sometimes conveyed in a litter, sometimes riding (since through the recent heavy rains it was more than ordinarily wearisome to ride the worst roads, soft with mud), was on her way to Hatfield. Through every town and village and hamlet she passed, the inhabitants came out to gaze upon the royal retinue. They cheered the

148

Queen and shouted their blessings, and often by her command the procession would slow down to crawling pace or altogether stop, while she smiled upon her people, or bent from her horse stripping her hand of its gauntlet glove that those who pressed near might kiss her white fingers. She had, said the older people who remembered earlier royal pilgrimages, all the graciousness and geniality of her famous father, Royal Harry—for it was as such that he was remembered, sorely though his taxes and the many tyrannies of his reign had oppressed high and low. He had had the gift of commanding popularity for which there was little justification, though without doubt he had been a colourful figure in his prime, and since then, in the reigns of his weak son and fanatically religious elder daughter, there had been a drabness and a lack of all careless joy. But the Queen, with her halo of fiery red hair, her white skin, her flashing eyes, was of the same mettle as her great father. As he had done, she readily received petitions, promising to consider them, and surprisingly some of the more reasonable were later granted. She exclaimed with pleasure over the children's gifts of posies from the cottage gardens and beckoned to an old woman on crutches, to ask what ailed her. Being told that it was the rheumatism, she bade one of those who rode beside her to give the poor dame money, so that she might have sufficient firing throughout the winter.

With such delays the journey was a slow one, and it was small wonder that the Queen was tired when she arrived at Hatfield. There would be several brief halts before she reached her journey's end, but Elizabeth loved these processions through rural England, and knew the value of personal appearances. It mattered nothing that some of her ladies, less addicted to travel, and less luxuriously lodged at the country mansions which were privileged to house the Queen for a night, secretly grumbled. Probably it rarely occurred to her that the expense of entertaining her even for a day and a night threw the finances of some of her less wealthy subjects into dire confusion. None the less the visit was an honour, coveted despite all its attendant expense, and thereafter none but the most noble guests would be allowed to sleep in the room or the bed where for a few hours the Queen had rested.

Erica, as she had feared, received only an hour's notice of

Elizabeth's visit. A gentleman in the royal retinue was sent ahead to give warning, and Erica could only surmise how long the visit would be likely to last. It was four hours past noon when the procession wound up the avenue, and Erica, spying it from an upstairs window, saw with relief that it was a short one. There were finely-clad riders, a half-score of them on either side of the Queen's litter, but no sign so far as Erica could see of any female attendant for which she was duly thankful. Menfolk were easily entertained, and she could leave that to her husband.

Although notice had been so short, banners and pennants furled out from the long avenue of trees, and there were more encircling the great front door. The members of the household were lined up on either side of it, and in the doorway, Sir Richard and Erica stood hand in hand, waiting to receive the Queen. As she was assisted from her litter they knelt before her. Elizabeth, extending her hand to both in turn, bade them rise, then turned that smiling gaze which never seemed to tire upon the assembled servants. Such was its charm that each felt they had been singled out for special recognition. She held Erica by the hand and kissed her on the cheek.

"But did you not receive our command that there was to be no festive display?" She inquired as in mild reproof.

"Your Majesty, can this be described as such?" Erica asked. "A few poor flags and gawds put up within the last hour."

The Queen smiled. "Ah well, let it pass, but we have had the longing that all should be as in the old days, when we were sore in need of loyal friendship, and you were but a girl bride. Now though you have, so we heard, two fine sons, you have changed little, Erica."

"Your Majesty has changed to a most wondrous beauty," Erica said—and sincerely, for there had been nothing of this dazzling quality in the fragile Lady Elizabeth, who although Queen Mary's sister, had lived in semi-imprisonment.

As vanity was perhaps the Queen's most human characteristic this pleased. The royal "we" was promptly dropped and she said: "I can stay but for a few hours, so let it be as though we meet as two old friends with my royal state forgot. There are few whom I would wish to treat me so

150

but you and your good husband have always had a place in my heart."

"And you the entire devotion of ours," Erica said.

So it was that presently they sat together, alone by royal request in Erica's boudoir, and Elizabeth spread out her slender, exquisite hands to the cheerful flames of the log fire. Her slender torso in its tight bodice rose like the calyx of a flower from the great spread of her nut-brown velvet skirts. She had always been fond of dark, rich colours and of velvet, Erica remembered; but there had also been a simplicity, and to-day she *was* simple. A square neckline and a rolled pointed collar instead of the fashionable ruff; no jewels save a few rings on her long fingers and a pearl-studded cross on a chain about her neck. Her red hair was dressed high. In the old days there had been a sickly tinge to her pallor, but to-day it glowed with the transparent effect of alabaster. They spoke of many things, which were mostly trivial and in the past but evoked laughter and a few sighs. Then at last the Queen said:

"My ward is still here, is she not—under your roof? She *is* my ward again, now that her husband is dead and she has no other protection. Strange tidings came to me in connection with Guy Erskine's death. The marriage, I hear, was unhappy."

Erica answered soberly: "Yes, Your Grace, it was excessively unhappy."

"Not only, I gather, because the child died. I heard of some trollop who made Morag's life a burden to her, and ruled that foolish, mad boy through his infatuation. I heard that as he lay dead, the tenantry, inflamed against his wife, rose up against her and would have drowned or burnt her as a witch, because of her modelling skill, which I had fostered. I heard that she faced the mob with courage, yet said that if die she must, it should be in such a way as should bring no retribution upon them, and that she was but rescued from her peril at the extreme hour of it. Is all this true?"

Yes, it was true, Erica assured her, and she added details, to the imperfect story that had been retailed to the Queen, who cried out, conscience-stricken: "Had I but known him for what he was, I would not have allowed this marriage, much less pressed it. God's truth, but one can be proud of

151

her; and, meek and gentle though she was, I am not wholly surprised, for there were times when I divined strength in her. Now I would see her, and be alone with her for a while."

Erica said smiling: "Morag waits without for such a summons, and I will fetch her, and then, if Your Grace will allow—some simple repast."

"So that it *is* simple," the Queen replied. "Your husband I make no doubt will see that my gentlemen are fed and wined, but for ourselves let it be no feast, only some small collation we can take of here together. To me it is a luxury almost unsurpassed to be simple, and there will be pomp and magnificence enough at my journey's end."

Morag knelt at the Queen's feet in her widow's black and though the setting was so different, she was strongly reminded of that first audience years ago when she had been a terrified yet hating child, with her whole mourning heart fixed on her who had been Amy Robsart, and later Dudley's neglected wife. She had known since, the humiliation that such neglect entailed, though it had been worse for her dear Amy, because Amy had loved her husband.

The Queen said with the gentleness, the sigh that was not unfamiliar: "There have been times when I have missed you, Morag. How has it been with you?"

"They have been bad times, Your Grace, and I have longed for the old days at Windsor—longed to see your smile, to hear your voice."

"My poor sweeting, in all unconsciousness I used you ill." Elizabeth impulsively stretched out her hands and lifted Morag to her feet. "Why, you are but feather-light," she said remorsefully, "and your face so pale and wan. Would that I had not sent you from me, or at the least had not commanded this marriage. Rather should you have gone to Holland as I once wished. It would have been better, would it not?"

"Much better, Your Majesty, if you were resolved to send me far away." Morag gazed at the well-remembered the incomparable face—not exactly beautiful, but so much more than beautiful; and now at last she knew that without doubt she loved the Queen.

"Sit in this low chair, drawn close to me," Elizabeth invited, "and there shall be truth between us. I had the

152

thought, the fear, that one for whom I cared much was drawn towards you, and for you it would have been possible to marry him, though for myself, for reasons of State, it was not. This must ne'er be spoken of again, Morag, between us, nor repeated outside this room."

"Never." Morag's voice was a thread of a whisper. "But Your Grace was mistaken—there was nobody."

The name which was in both their minds was not uttered. At the time when jealousy had tormented Elizabeth, there had been still the thought that one day she might marry Dudley, but every day since then the possibility had become more remote. The truth she had faced and acknowledged. She had no taste for marriage; would still have had no taste for it even had she been beloved by a King as great as herself—one who was rich, handsome, powerful and chivalrous, endowed with all the virtues. She would rule alone, and rule successfully, and in days to come men would say that she had been the greatest Tudor of them all. It was an ease to the heart that the passion between herself and Dudley had waned, though he was still in his way devoted to her, and she would always have a special fondness for him. He was the Earl of Leicester now, and in time to come, because of that fondness there would be further honours and rewards she would bestow on him. Presently Elizabeth tossed his name into the conversation, as though it was of no account. Morag understood now. The Queen must have witnessed that one hot embrace; it was this that had brought disaster upon her. This brief encounter with Robert Dudley seemed a lifetime away, and she could only wonder at the ardour he had aroused in her.

The Queen questioned her and she answered the questions with a veracious simplicity. She did not traduce Guy, but said that she had been almost as sorry for him as for herself. She could not be led to graphic descriptions of the dreadful night when she had outfaced the mob who had sought to kill her, but none the less the Queen was greatly stirred. She clasped Morag's hands closely in hers, and said tautly that had she known earlier, no forgiving prayers should have saved them; one and all should at the least have suffered a sound whipping.

"And now, what of yourself?" Elizabeth said presently. "These good people here would keep you with them for as long as you care to stay, but it may be that you would prefer to be at court again, and this time in a more important position; or if you so wish, you can still study in Amsterdam, and become perhaps a great sculptor."

Morag was silent, sitting with her head bent and her eyes fixed on the beautiful hands that clasped hers. She said: "Before I accept aught else from Your Majesty, there is a thing I must tell you, that I should have told you long since, when I was a child and you were graciously kind to me. I did try——" Morag raised her face and her eyes were earnest. " 'Twas on my wedding eve, but you were asleep, having suffered all the day from a headache and Mrs. Ashley would not have me disturb you."

"What secret thing could you have had to tell, save perchance that you had given your heart to another?"

"But I had not given it—then."

Although the last word was an unconscious betrayal, the Queen took no open note of it, but waited quietly, with the patience that was often in evidence when her ministers put a problem before her or urged advice, and was at least as familiar to them as her outbursts of imperious disagreement. Morag continued painfully:

"When I was first brought to court, as a child, it was to question me, to try to force from me that Amy Dudley, my cousin, had oft threatened to take her own life. Mayhap it was surmised that I had witnessed it, and that shock and terror had tied my tongue; but it was not so. Your Majesty, one can be sore of heart as she was, and yet there can still be the joy of living, and the hope that in the end there will be happiness. I have felt this myself, and it was so with her."

"Wouldst tell me then that after all she was murdered, and that you saw the crime committed?"

"Oh no, no! Though I was wicked enough to hope sometimes that you would believe it, and punish him—her lord. Because of her there was a hatred in my heart that I dared not show. . . . She had known much grief, suffered much unkindness, but for her death none was to blame . . . only a strange malaise which she concealed from all save myself."

The Queen said thoughtfully: "Rumour had it that there was a tumour of the breast, but the autopsy revealed none."

"She had fits of dizziness, Your Grace, when her sight and her mind too were clouded. On recovery she could not remember what had happened, only that for a while there had been naught but blankness. Only the day before she died, when we were alone together, she fell down the terrace steps. 'Twas not a dangerous fall and the sward was soft, but as I knelt beside her I thought her dead, and would have run for help, but that she opened her eyes and seemed none the worse, and again bade me tell no one. But when the next day she was found at the foot of the great stairs, why then —why then I knew I should have told . . . and that through my silence I had lost her, so dear to me. . . . I hid—my grief seemed more than I could bear. . . ."

"When my Lord Dudley questioned you, when I questioned you, you were mute," mused Elizabeth, "and that was for hatred's sake. . . ."

"I was but a child," Morag faltered, "and afterwards I was sorry, but knew not how to tell. That last night at Windsor, then I would . . . but it was too late, I could not see you. . . ."

"Even had you done so it was mayhap too late—for me," said Elizabeth.

The thought came to her that she should be grateful for Morag's silence, since at the time of Amy's death she had never better loved Robert Dudley, and for that love might have braved an unpopular marriage which would have angered the people and turned their hearts against her. The cause of Amy's death might have been given some credence, for Morag would have borne public witness to it, yet there would have been many to say that a child's evidence could be forced. Since those days a Queen had learnt a queenly wisdom, though even then in her secret heart she had known that marriage was not for her.

"I have much thankfulness," said Elizabeth, "that I never doubted him."

"Can Your Grace find it in your heart to forgive me?" Morag entreated.

"Who can persist in anger against a child? You loved her much, and would have avenged her sorrow." The Queen's hand dropped on Morag's shoulder, and she twisted around her head to kiss it.

"In my own time, I will tell Robin of this," Elizabeth

155

said. "He is not with me on this journey, but in Ireland, where there has been much trouble of late. Now again, as I told Erica Adrian, you are the Queen's ward, and I would have you happy. A place at court—that you shall have, if it is what your heart covets, or the sculptor's training in Holland. The choice is yours."

"May I . . . would Your Grace give time to consider?"

"That I will—and gladly, if only to atone for the little time given you before I had you married. Perchance in your mind you harbour some other plan."

"No-o, but . . ." Morag's cheeks had flushed and there was a glow in her eyes.

She was a pretty creature, thought Elizabeth, now that the wan pallor had lifted, and it was surely unlikely that during her unhappy marriage no man had been stirred by sympathy and a wish to rescue her from her plight. The girl had good judgement, and Elizabeth did not fear that given a free choice she would make a mistake in her man. But if love was even now in her heart, it was a timorous love—love in its first bloom, which even a light touch might bruise or damage.

"Whatsoever may betide, we shall not again be parted for so long," said Elizabeth, "though now time draws on, and I must soon leave."

"Erica," said Morag, "will fret if Your Majesty does so without wine or food."

"Then call her, child, for I promised her. . . ."

Morag got to her feet and ran to open the door. Servants who had been hovering brought in loaded trays, and Erica followed behind them.

Before that wonderful visit ended, the Queen insisted on seeing both Joan and Emmie, and gave them gracious praise for all they had done for Morag, whom she spoke of as her beloved ward. The two girls were both overwhelmed. It was a moment they would never forget.

"There is none like her. No Queen was ever so human or so great," Erica said, standing without the house to watch the cavalcade disappear down the avenue. Sir Richard, by the Queen's request, rode with her escort to Hatfield, and when he returned it was with miniatures of herself for Erica and for Morag.

The next day the Queen was again on her way, but for days to come it seemed as if none could talk of anything but her charm, her graciousness, her strange, compelling beauty.

Morag, however, had the breathless sense of waiting, and she could come to no decision betwen the choice of a court appointment and a sojourn in Holland. Stephen had written to her, and had said he would hope to see her before long, therefore it should have been no surprise when on a cold winter day, with snow threatening, he arrived on horseback, having because of the inclement weather been obliged to break his journey for two nights on the road.

Erica brought him to Morag in the oak parlour and left them together, and Morag, rising to greet him, was aware that this was an even greater moment in her life than the occasion of the Queen's visit. Yet she could think of nothing to say after the first formal words of greeting, and only stood there gazing at him with her great eyes.

" You have endured so much, would God I could have saved you from it, or that you could have called upon me," Stephen said.

" An it had been possible, so would I have done," Morag murmured.

For a silent minute they scanned each other. He had been in her dreams and in her thoughts, and it had been her consolation to recall each line of his face, to remember its kindness: the firmness of mouth and jaw and the smile which was more often in his eyes than on his lips.

" Your leg, has it quite mended?" she asked ineptly.

It was as good now as it had ever been, Stephen told her, finding a sweetness in her shyness, which was rather that of a maid than of one who had been wed, who had borne a child, and was now widowed. She looked, if anything, younger than she had looked on that never-to-be-forgotten day in the bluebell wood, for although she had passed through tribulation, the peace and sense of freedom of the last weeks had done much for her. From the moment he had received Erica's letter telling him of Guy's death and the peril that had threatened Morag, he had yearned to come to her, but prudence had conquered impetuosity. She must at least be given a short while to pay respect to her husband's memory, bad husband though he had been. Even now there should be no second hasty marriage, for although to him it was as though he knew her as well as he knew himself, he could not suppose that for her there was an equal sense of dear familiarity.

"When we met last," said Stephen, "we spoke of friendship, that precious gift; and you, accepting it, said it was as if we both lived again in King Arthur's day. That was a poetical turn of thought, but what I felt for you was real. It has lived in my mind ever since. How is it with you?"

"I—how can I say? It was a dream to me, which broke through the nightmares that followed after you left. When I was most miserable I thought of you, but yet I was so apart. I was—his, and my dead babe was his, and though I hoped to see the Queen, and would have prayed to her to have set me free, I wonder now if it could have been a real freedom while he still lived. But now the sundering is—absolute, and with each day that passes the memory becomes more dim. It is as though a curtain falls which will cut me off from the past."

"And then—when it has fallen, you will turn about to face a new future?"

"It must be so, Stephen, for how could one who is young live, mayhap, for years with a nightmare? Have we not all some right to seek the sun?"

"Every right, and I pray that you may seek it with me."

A shade of frowning trouble passed across her brow. "It would—it would be a grief not to give you happiness; and in all my life I have given so little; only for a short while to Amy. . . ."

"Because her alone you loved. . . ."

"Yes, but there is affection, Stephen, and loyalty, and that I owe to Joan and Emmie, who both strove to save my life. I cannot send them away from me, so long as they wish to stay."

"Why should you? In London, in the home we can share together, there would be room for them. Not in the old house where I at present live, but in one of the outlying villages such as Kensington village, where the fields are green, and there are flowers in abundance, and the houses are roomy with the sun pouring into them. . . ."

Morag's laughter broke then, though it was a tremulous

laughter. "You speak, as though 'tis already arranged that we shall marry."

"And is it not so—in our hearts? I spoke of friendship, but in sooth I loved you with my whole heart, and methinks there was at least some little love in yours."

"Dear Stephen, I dared not to examine my heart."

He laid an arm about her shoulders and drew her near to him. "But now you will?"

With a sigh of much content she rested her head upon his shoulder. "Aye, now I will," she promised.